DREAM

KUNG FU PANDA

ART OF BALANCE

APE ENTERTAINMENT

David Hedgecock
Co-Publisher / General Partner
DHedgecock@Ape-Entertainment.com

Brent E. Erwin
Co-Publisher / General Partner
BErwin@Ape-Entertainment.com

Jason M. Burns
Editor-in-Chief
JBurns@Ape-Entertainment.com

Kevin Freeman
Managing Editor
KFreeman@Ape-Entertainment.com

Matt Anderson
Assistant Editor
MAnderson@Ape-Entertainment.com

Troy Dye
Submissions Editor
TDye@Ape-Entertainment.com

Steve Bryant
Designer
SBryant@Ape-Entertainment.com

Ape Entertainment
P.O. Box 7100
San Diego, CA 92167
www.ApeComics.com

APE DIGITAL COMIC SITE:
Apecmx.com

TWITTER:
Twitter.com/ApeComics

FACEBOOK:
Facebook.com/pages/Ape-Entertainment

MYSPACE:
MySpace.com/ApeEntertainment

To find more great
DreamWorks Animation
comics, visit us
on the web at
Kizoic.com

THE ART OF BALANCE

Written by:
Matt Anderson

Art/Colors by:
Dan Schoening

ONE SET OF HORNS

Written by:
Len Wallace

Art/Colors by:
Christine Larsen

THE DRAGON CHEF

Written by:
Jim Hankins

Art by:
Dario Brizuela

Colors by:
CV Design

THE TOUCH OF DESTINY

Written by:
Quinn Johnson

Art by:
Chris Houghton

Colors by:
Diego Rodriguez

Cover by: **Rolando Mallada**

Letters by: **David Hedgecock**

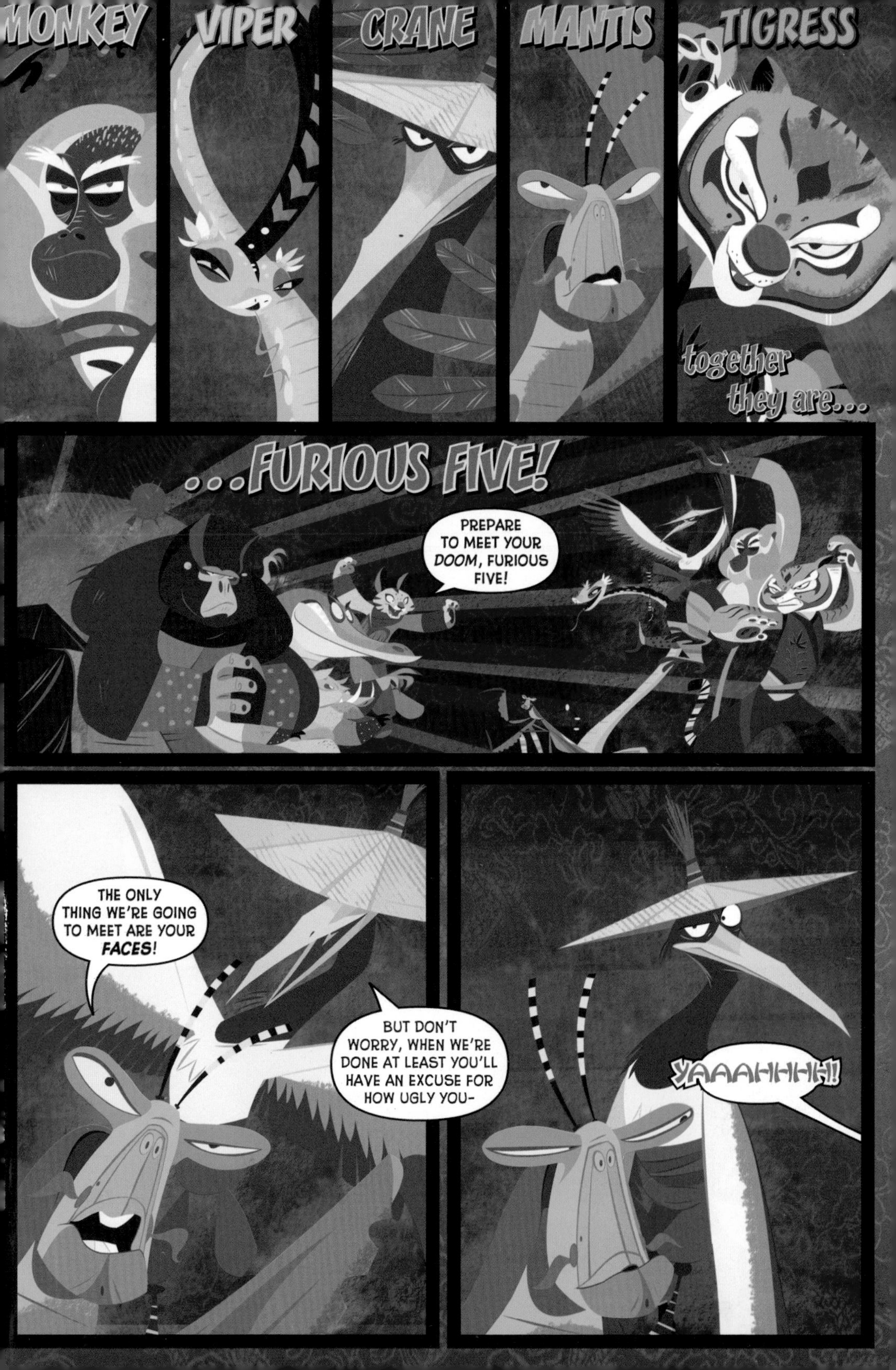
MONKEY
VIPER
CRANE
MANTIS
TIGRESS
together they are...
...FURIOUS FIVE!
PREPARE TO MEET YOUR DOOM, FURIOUS FIVE!
THE ONLY THING WE'RE GOING TO MEET ARE YOUR FACES!
BUT DON'T WORRY, WHEN WE'RE DONE AT LEAST YOU'LL HAVE AN EXCUSE FOR HOW UGLY YOU-
YAAAHHHH!

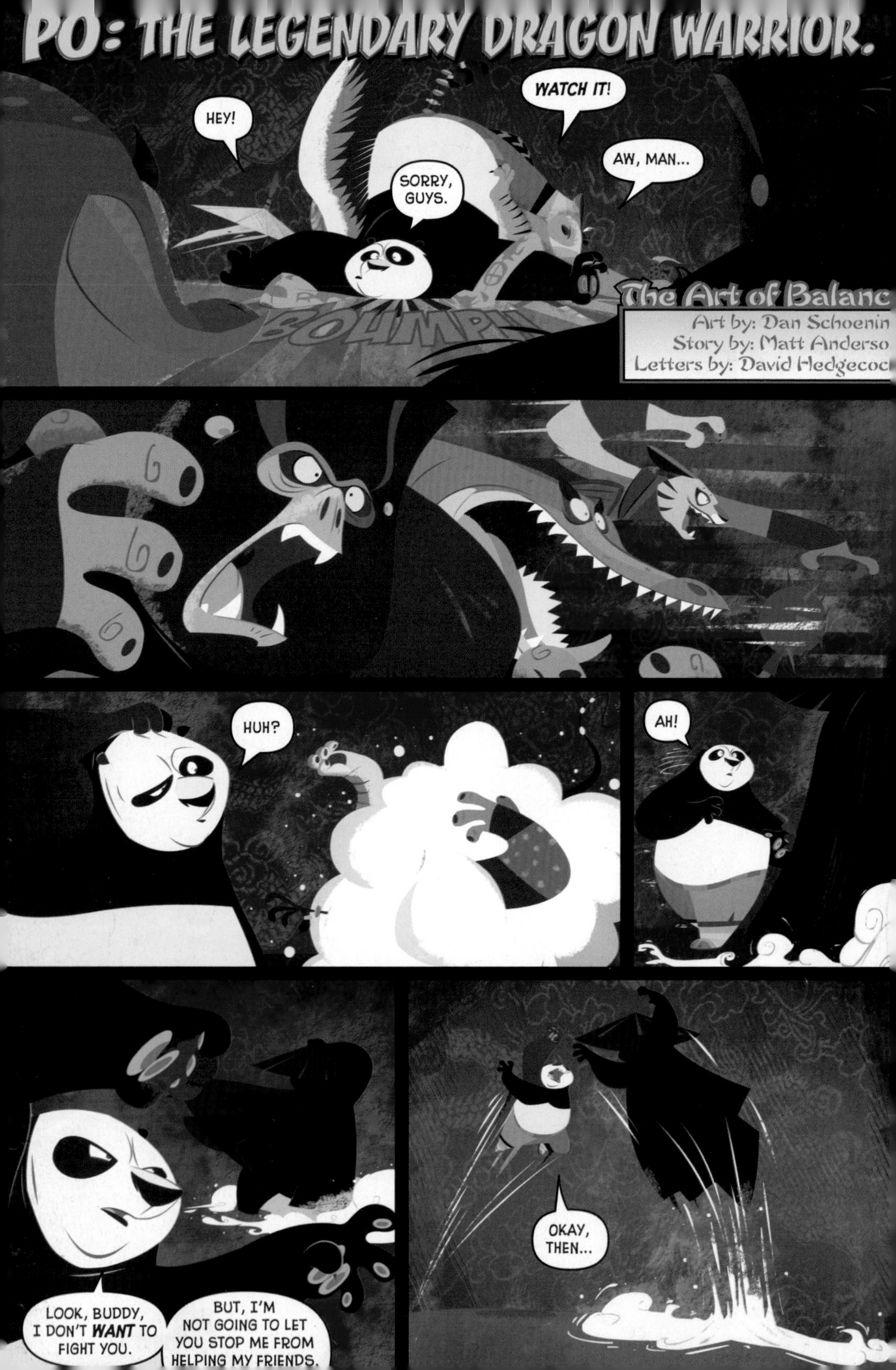
PO: THE LEGENDARY DRAGON WARRIOR.
HEY!
WATCH IT!
AW, MAN...
SORRY, GUYS.
BOHMPH
The Art of Balanc
Art by: Dan Schoenin
Story by: Matt Anderso
Letters by: David Hedgecoc
HUH?
AH!
LOOK, BUDDY, I DON'T WANT TO FIGHT YOU.
BUT, I'M NOT GOING TO LET YOU STOP ME FROM HELPING MY FRIENDS.
OKAY, THEN...

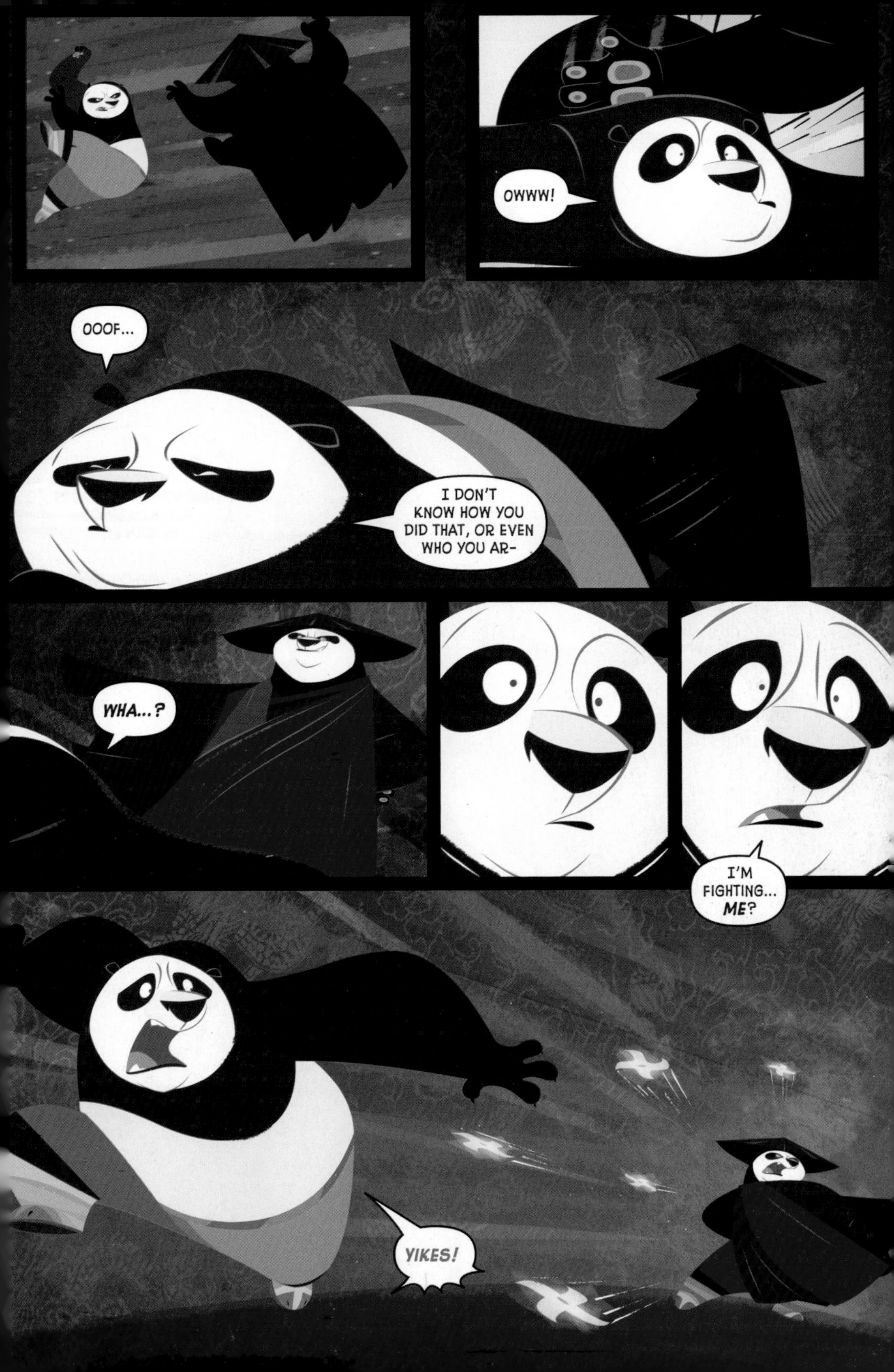
OWWW!
OOOF...
I DON'T KNOW HOW YOU DID THAT, OR EVEN WHO YOU AR-
WHA...?
I'M FIGHTING... ME?
YIKES!

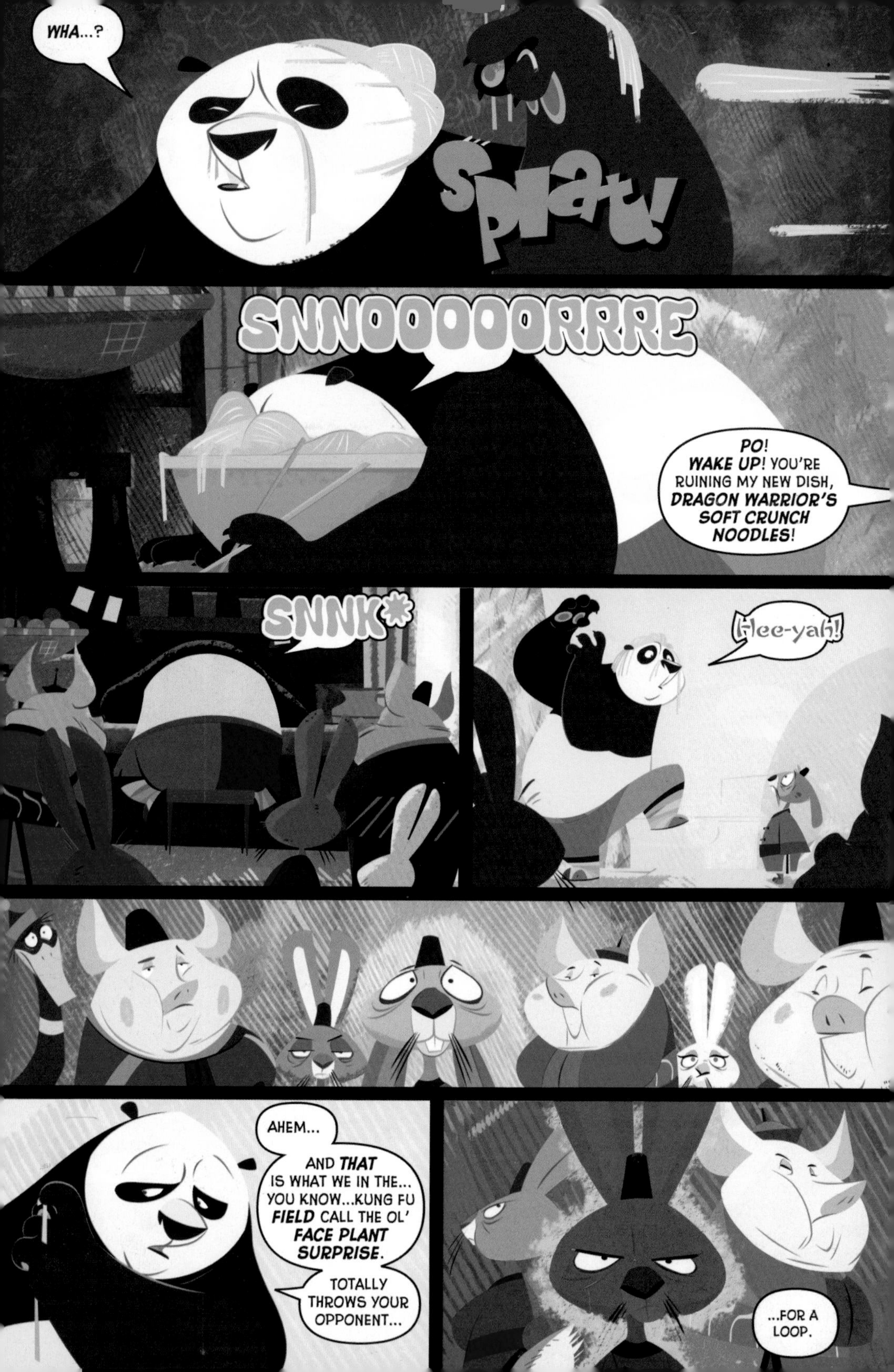
WHA...?
SPLAT!
SNNOOOOORRRE
PO! WAKE UP! YOU'RE RUINING MY NEW DISH, DRAGON WARRIOR'S SOFT CRUNCH NOODLES!
SNNK*
Hee-yah!
AHEM...
AND THAT IS WHAT WE IN THE... YOU KNOW...KUNG FU FIELD CALL THE OL' FACE PLANT SURPRISE.
TOTALLY THROWS YOUR OPPONENT...
...FOR A LOOP.

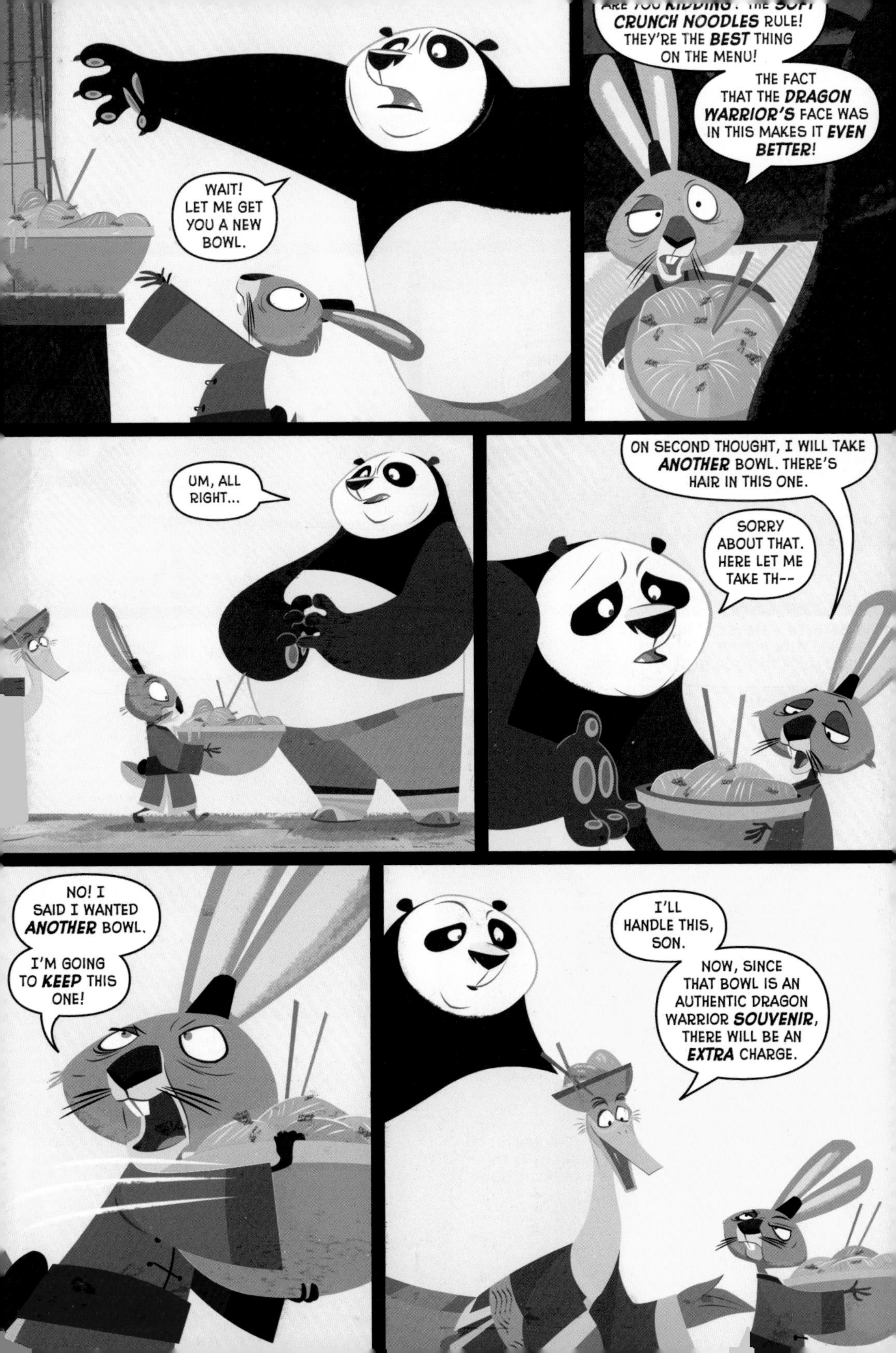
WAIT! LET ME GET YOU A NEW BOWL.
CRUNCH NOODLES RULE! THEY'RE THE BEST THING ON THE MENU!
THE FACT THAT THE DRAGON WARRIOR'S FACE WAS IN THIS MAKES IT EVEN BETTER!
UM, ALL RIGHT...
ON SECOND THOUGHT, I WILL TAKE ANOTHER BOWL. THERE'S HAIR IN THIS ONE.
SORRY ABOUT THAT. HERE LET ME TAKE TH--
NO! I SAID I WANTED ANOTHER BOWL.
I'M GOING TO KEEP THIS ONE!
I'LL HANDLE THIS, SON.
NOW, SINCE THAT BOWL IS AN AUTHENTIC DRAGON WARRIOR SOUVENIR, THERE WILL BE AN EXTRA CHARGE.

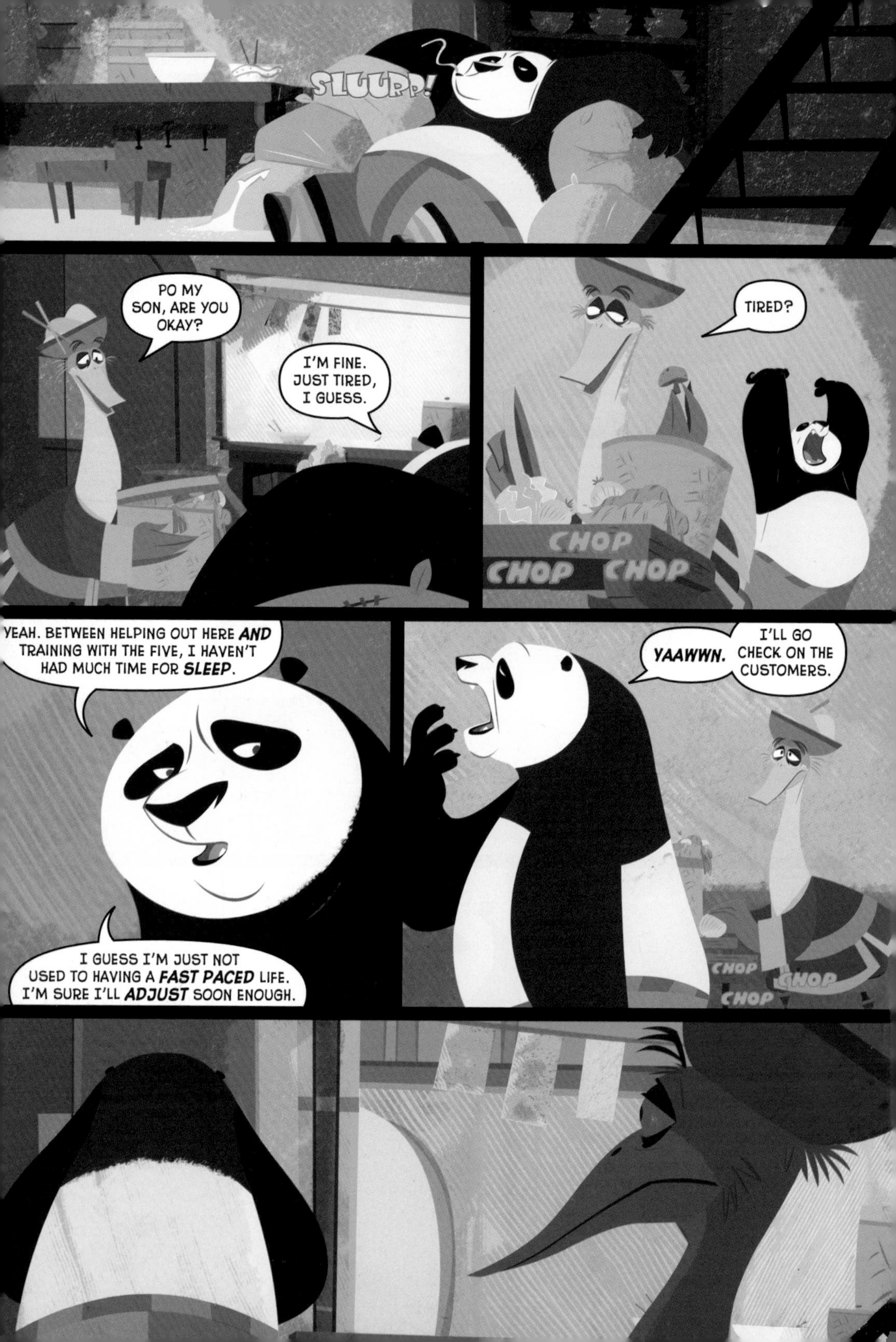
SLUURP!
PO MY SON, ARE YOU OKAY?
I'M FINE. JUST TIRED, I GUESS.
TIRED?
CHOP
CHOP
CHOP
YEAH. BETWEEN HELPING OUT HERE AND TRAINING WITH THE FIVE, I HAVEN'T HAD MUCH TIME FOR SLEEP.
I GUESS I'M JUST NOT USED TO HAVING A FAST PACED LIFE. I'M SURE I'LL ADJUST SOON ENOUGH.
YAAWWN.
I'LL GO CHECK ON THE CUSTOMERS.
CHOP
CHOP
CHOP

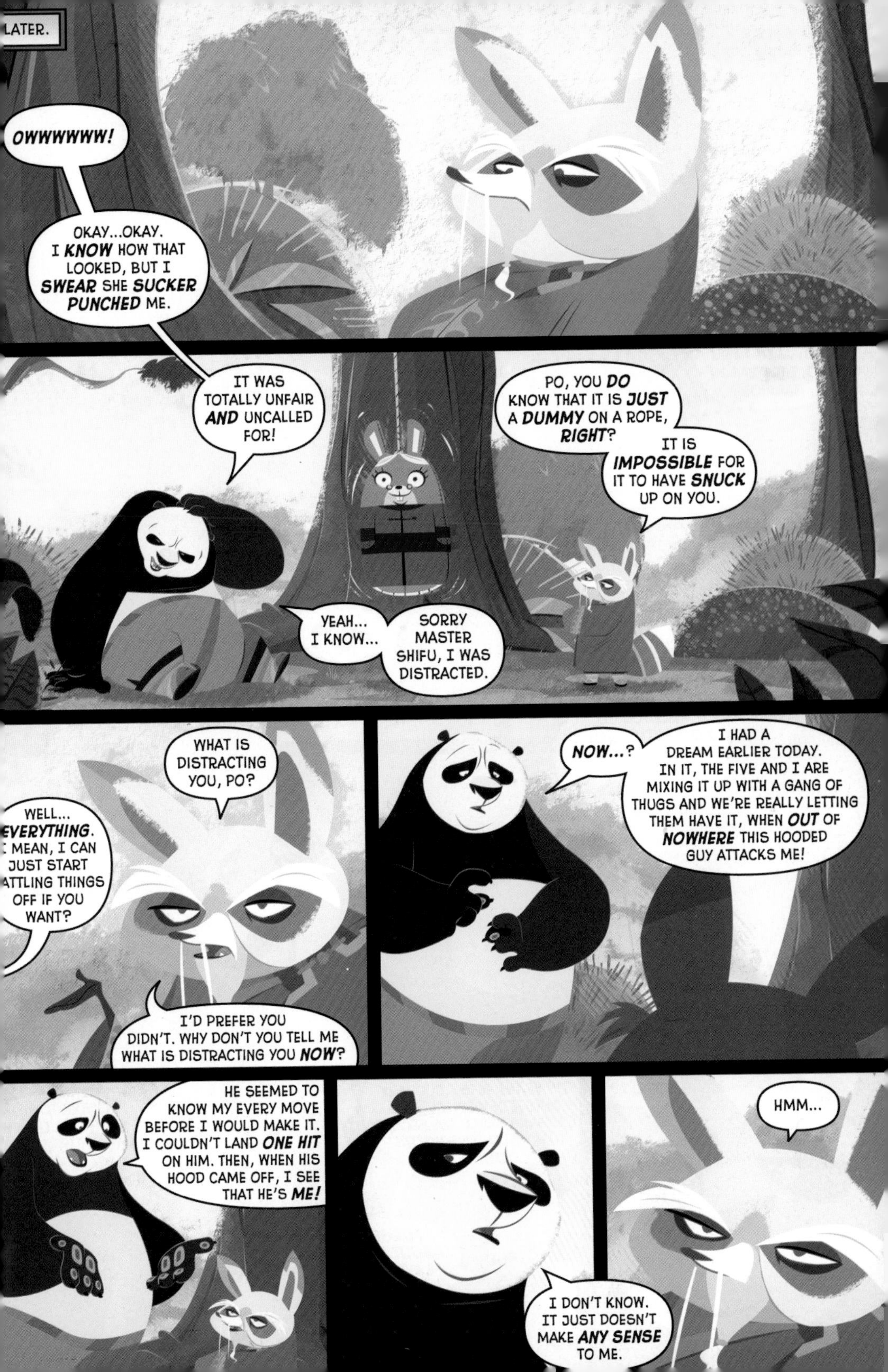
LATER.
OWWWWWW!
OKAY...OKAY. I KNOW HOW THAT LOOKED, BUT I SWEAR SHE SUCKER PUNCHED ME.
IT WAS TOTALLY UNFAIR AND UNCALLED FOR!
PO, YOU DO KNOW THAT IT IS JUST A DUMMY ON A ROPE, RIGHT?
IT IS IMPOSSIBLE FOR IT TO HAVE SNUCK UP ON YOU.
YEAH... I KNOW...
SORRY MASTER SHIFU, I WAS DISTRACTED.
WHAT IS DISTRACTING YOU, PO?
WELL... EVERYTHING. I MEAN, I CAN JUST START ATTLING THINGS OFF IF YOU WANT?
I'D PREFER YOU DIDN'T. WHY DON'T YOU TELL ME WHAT IS DISTRACTING YOU NOW?
NOW...?
I HAD A DREAM EARLIER TODAY. IN IT, THE FIVE AND I ARE MIXING IT UP WITH A GANG OF THUGS AND WE'RE REALLY LETTING THEM HAVE IT, WHEN OUT OF NOWHERE THIS HOODED GUY ATTACKS ME!
HE SEEMED TO KNOW MY EVERY MOVE BEFORE I WOULD MAKE IT. I COULDN'T LAND ONE HIT ON HIM. THEN, WHEN HIS HOOD CAME OFF, I SEE THAT HE'S ME!
I DON'T KNOW. IT JUST DOESN'T MAKE ANY SENSE TO ME.
HMM...

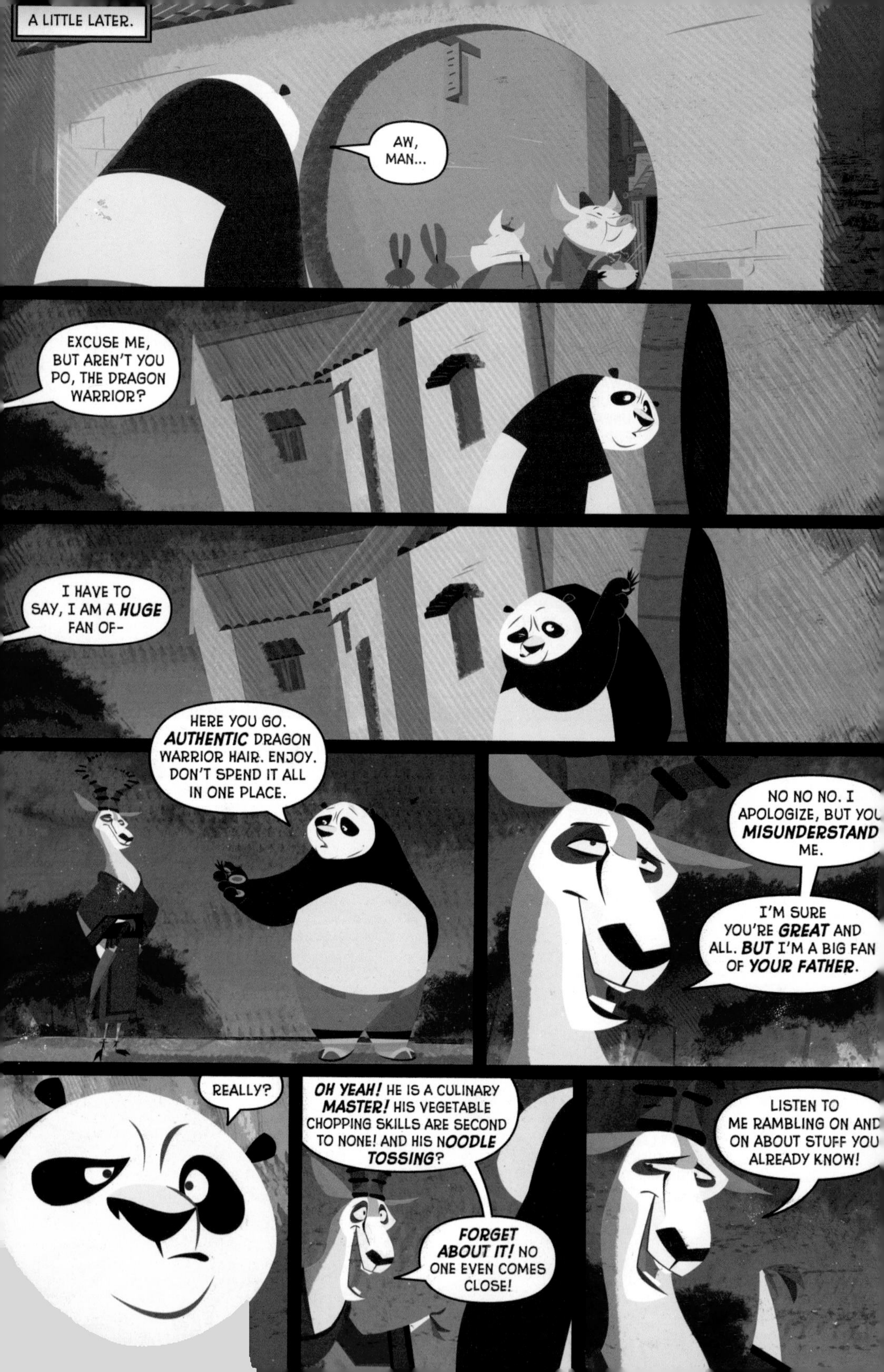
A LITTLE LATER.
AW, MAN...
EXCUSE ME, BUT AREN'T YOU PO, THE DRAGON WARRIOR?
I HAVE TO SAY, I AM A HUGE FAN OF-
HERE YOU GO. AUTHENTIC DRAGON WARRIOR HAIR. ENJOY. DON'T SPEND IT ALL IN ONE PLACE.
NO NO NO. I APOLOGIZE, BUT YOU MISUNDERSTAND ME.
I'M SURE YOU'RE GREAT AND ALL. BUT I'M A BIG FAN OF YOUR FATHER.
REALLY?
OH YEAH! HE IS A CULINARY MASTER! HIS VEGETABLE CHOPPING SKILLS ARE SECOND TO NONE! AND HIS NOODLE TOSSING?
FORGET ABOUT IT! NO ONE EVEN COMES CLOSE!
LISTEN TO ME RAMBLING ON AND ON ABOUT STUFF YOU ALREADY KNOW!

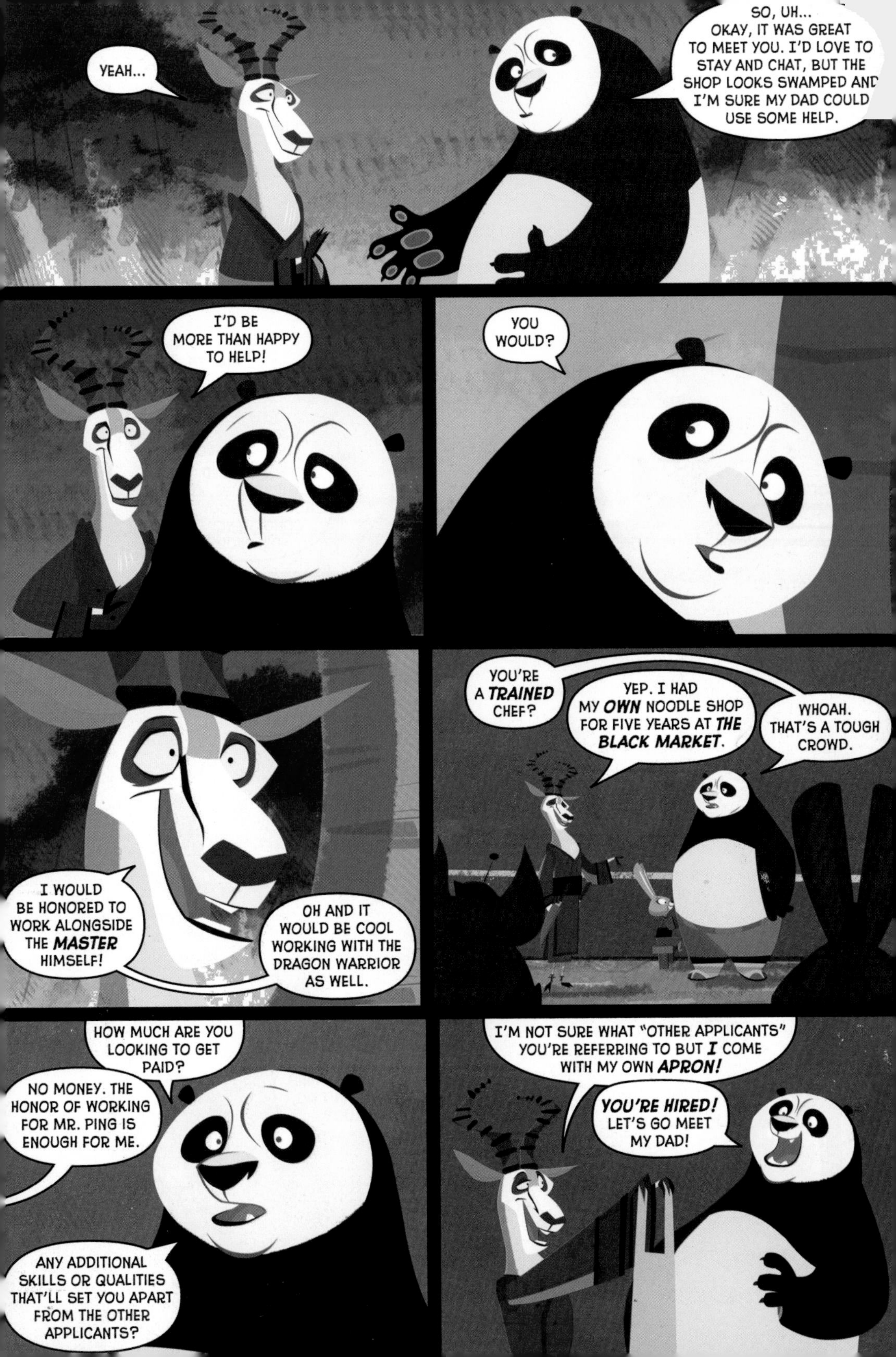
YEAH...
SO, UH... OKAY, IT WAS GREAT TO MEET YOU. I'D LOVE TO STAY AND CHAT, BUT THE SHOP LOOKS SWAMPED AND I'M SURE MY DAD COULD USE SOME HELP.
I'D BE MORE THAN HAPPY TO HELP!
YOU WOULD?
I WOULD BE HONORED TO WORK ALONGSIDE THE **MASTER** HIMSELF!
OH AND IT WOULD BE COOL WORKING WITH THE DRAGON WARRIOR AS WELL.
YOU'RE A **TRAINED** CHEF?
YEP. I HAD MY **OWN** NOODLE SHOP FOR FIVE YEARS AT **THE BLACK MARKET**.
WHOAH. THAT'S A TOUGH CROWD.
HOW MUCH ARE YOU LOOKING TO GET PAID?
NO MONEY. THE HONOR OF WORKING FOR MR. PING IS ENOUGH FOR ME.
ANY ADDITIONAL SKILLS OR QUALITIES THAT'LL SET YOU APART FROM THE OTHER APPLICANTS?
I'M NOT SURE WHAT "OTHER APPLICANTS" YOU'RE REFERRING TO BUT **I** COME WITH MY OWN **APRON!**
YOU'RE HIRED! LET'S GO MEET MY DAD!

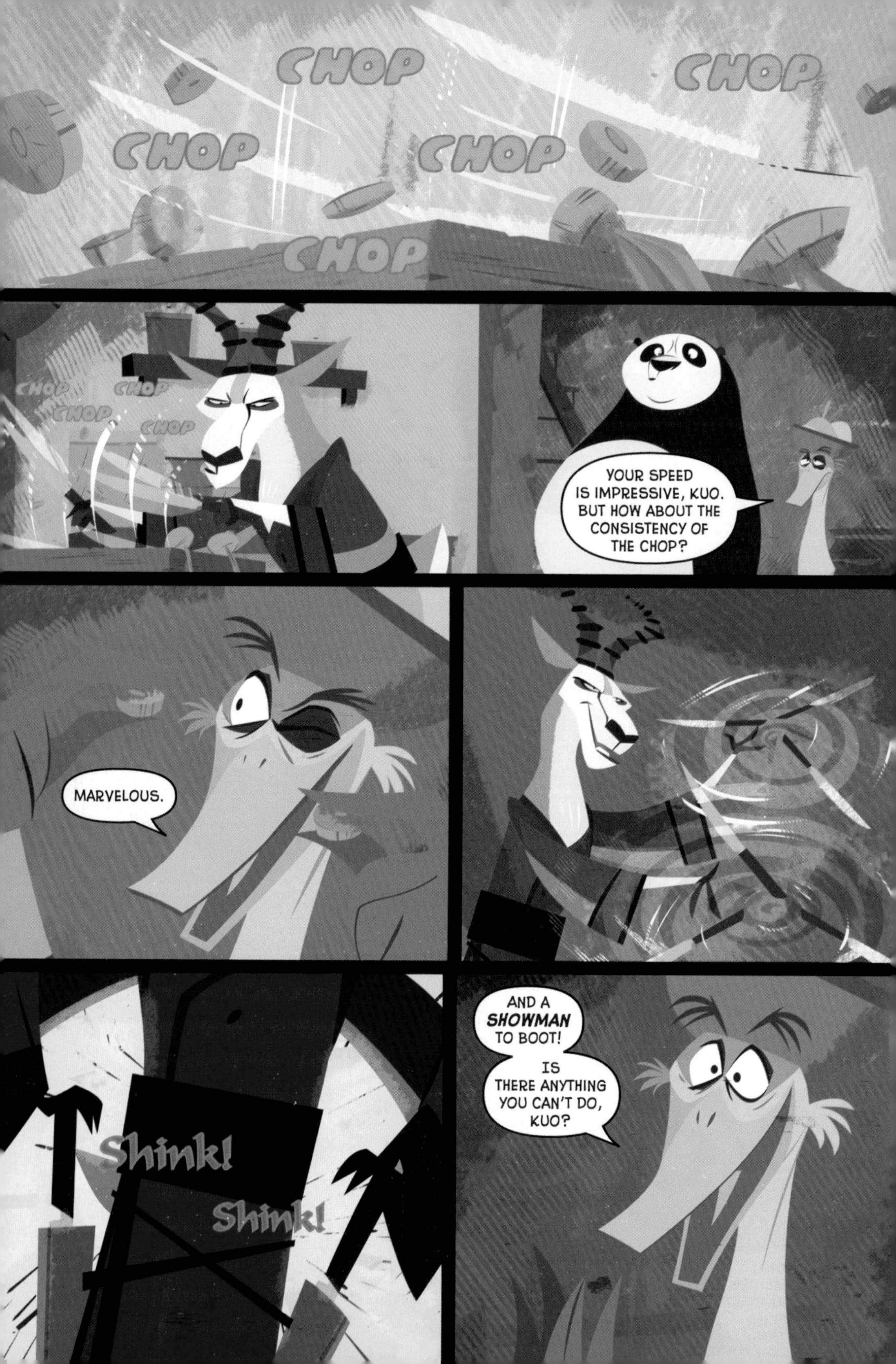
CHOP
CHOP
CHOP
CHOP
CHOP
CHOP
CHOP
CHOP
CHOP
YOUR SPEED IS IMPRESSIVE, KUO. BUT HOW ABOUT THE CONSISTENCY OF THE CHOP?
MARVELOUS.
Shink!
Shink!
AND A SHOWMAN TO BOOT!
IS THERE ANYTHING YOU CAN'T DO, KUO?

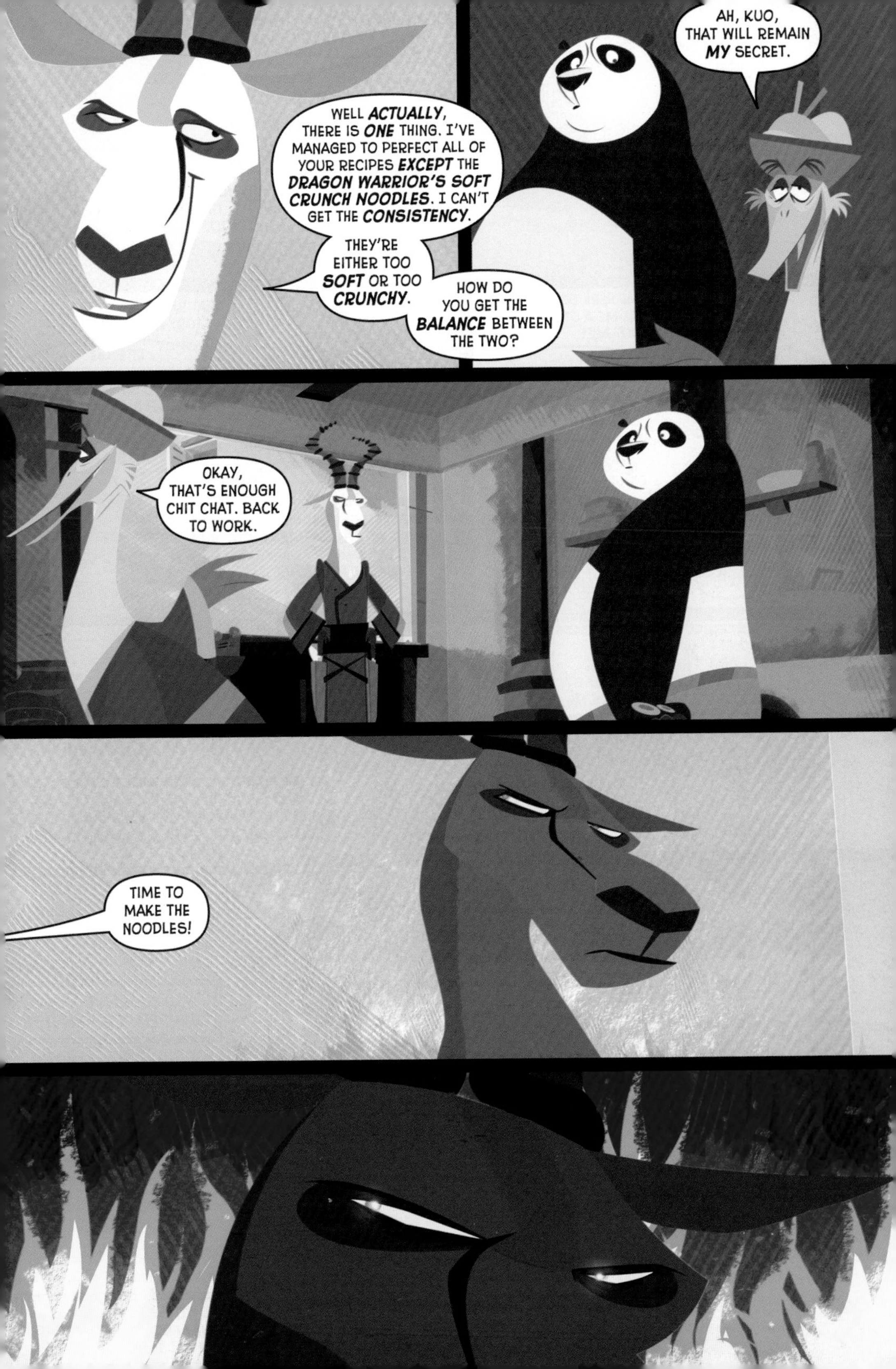
WELL ACTUALLY, THERE IS ONE THING. I'VE MANAGED TO PERFECT ALL OF YOUR RECIPES EXCEPT THE DRAGON WARRIOR'S SOFT CRUNCH NOODLES. I CAN'T GET THE CONSISTENCY.
THEY'RE EITHER TOO SOFT OR TOO CRUNCHY.
HOW DO YOU GET THE BALANCE BETWEEN THE TWO?
AH, KUO, THAT WILL REMAIN MY SECRET.
OKAY, THAT'S ENOUGH CHIT CHAT. BACK TO WORK.
TIME TO MAKE THE NOODLES!

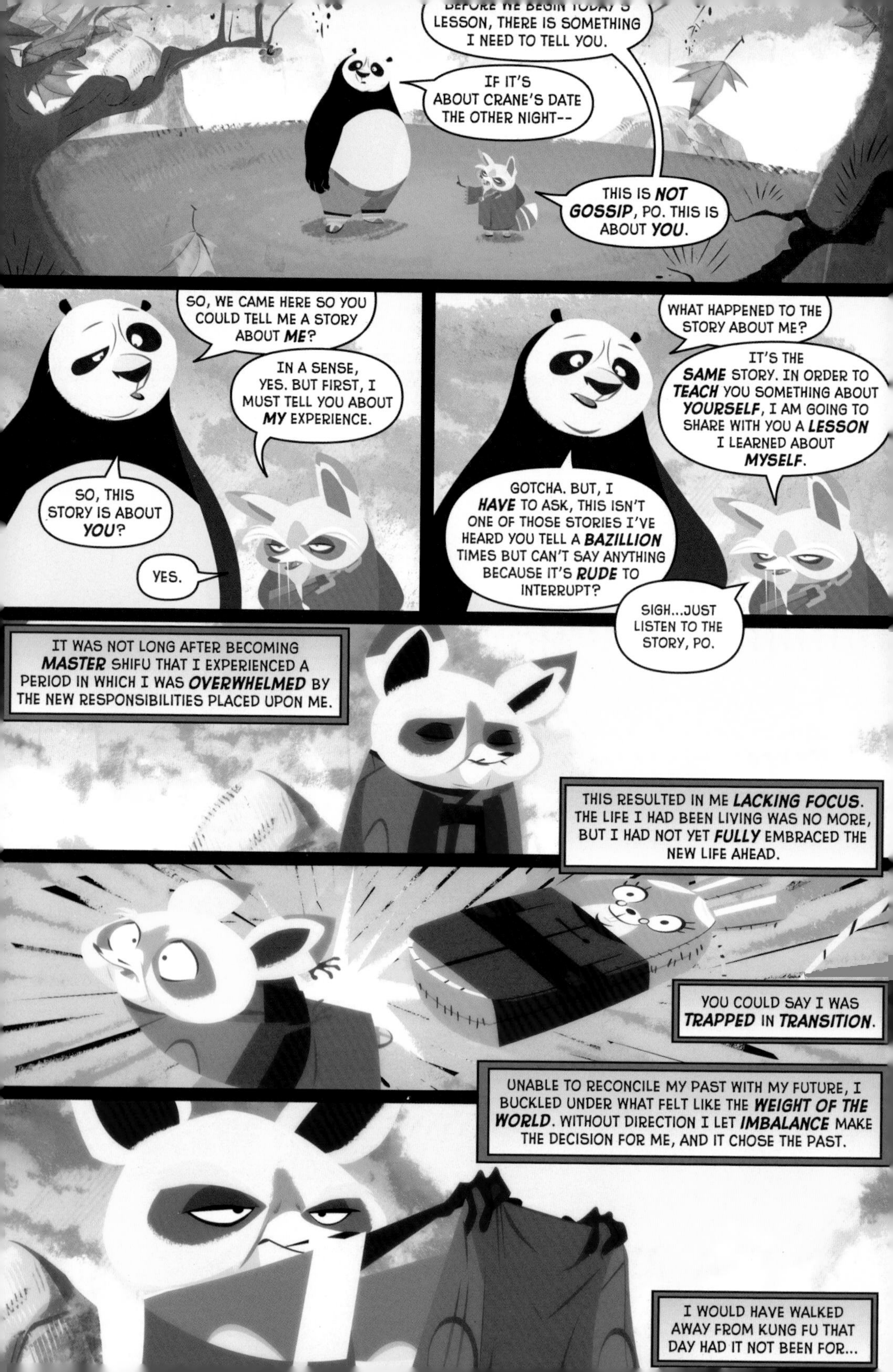

BEFORE WE BEGIN TODAY'S LESSON, THERE IS SOMETHING I NEED TO TELL YOU.
IF IT'S ABOUT CRANE'S DATE THE OTHER NIGHT--
THIS IS NOT GOSSIP, PO. THIS IS ABOUT YOU.
SO, WE CAME HERE SO YOU COULD TELL ME A STORY ABOUT ME?
IN A SENSE, YES. BUT FIRST, I MUST TELL YOU ABOUT MY EXPERIENCE.
SO, THIS STORY IS ABOUT YOU?
YES.
WHAT HAPPENED TO THE STORY ABOUT ME?
IT'S THE SAME STORY. IN ORDER TO TEACH YOU SOMETHING ABOUT YOURSELF, I AM GOING TO SHARE WITH YOU A LESSON I LEARNED ABOUT MYSELF.
GOTCHA. BUT, I HAVE TO ASK, THIS ISN'T ONE OF THOSE STORIES I'VE HEARD YOU TELL A BAZILLION TIMES BUT CAN'T SAY ANYTHING BECAUSE IT'S RUDE TO INTERRUPT?
SIGH...JUST LISTEN TO THE STORY, PO.
IT WAS NOT LONG AFTER BECOMING MASTER SHIFU THAT I EXPERIENCED A PERIOD IN WHICH I WAS OVERWHELMED BY THE NEW RESPONSIBILITIES PLACED UPON ME.
THIS RESULTED IN ME LACKING FOCUS. THE LIFE I HAD BEEN LIVING WAS NO MORE, BUT I HAD NOT YET FULLY EMBRACED THE NEW LIFE AHEAD.
YOU COULD SAY I WAS TRAPPED IN TRANSITION.
UNABLE TO RECONCILE MY PAST WITH MY FUTURE, I BUCKLED UNDER WHAT FELT LIKE THE WEIGHT OF THE WORLD. WITHOUT DIRECTION I LET IMBALANCE MAKE THE DECISION FOR ME, AND IT CHOSE THE PAST.
I WOULD HAVE WALKED AWAY FROM KUNG FU THAT DAY HAD IT NOT BEEN FOR...

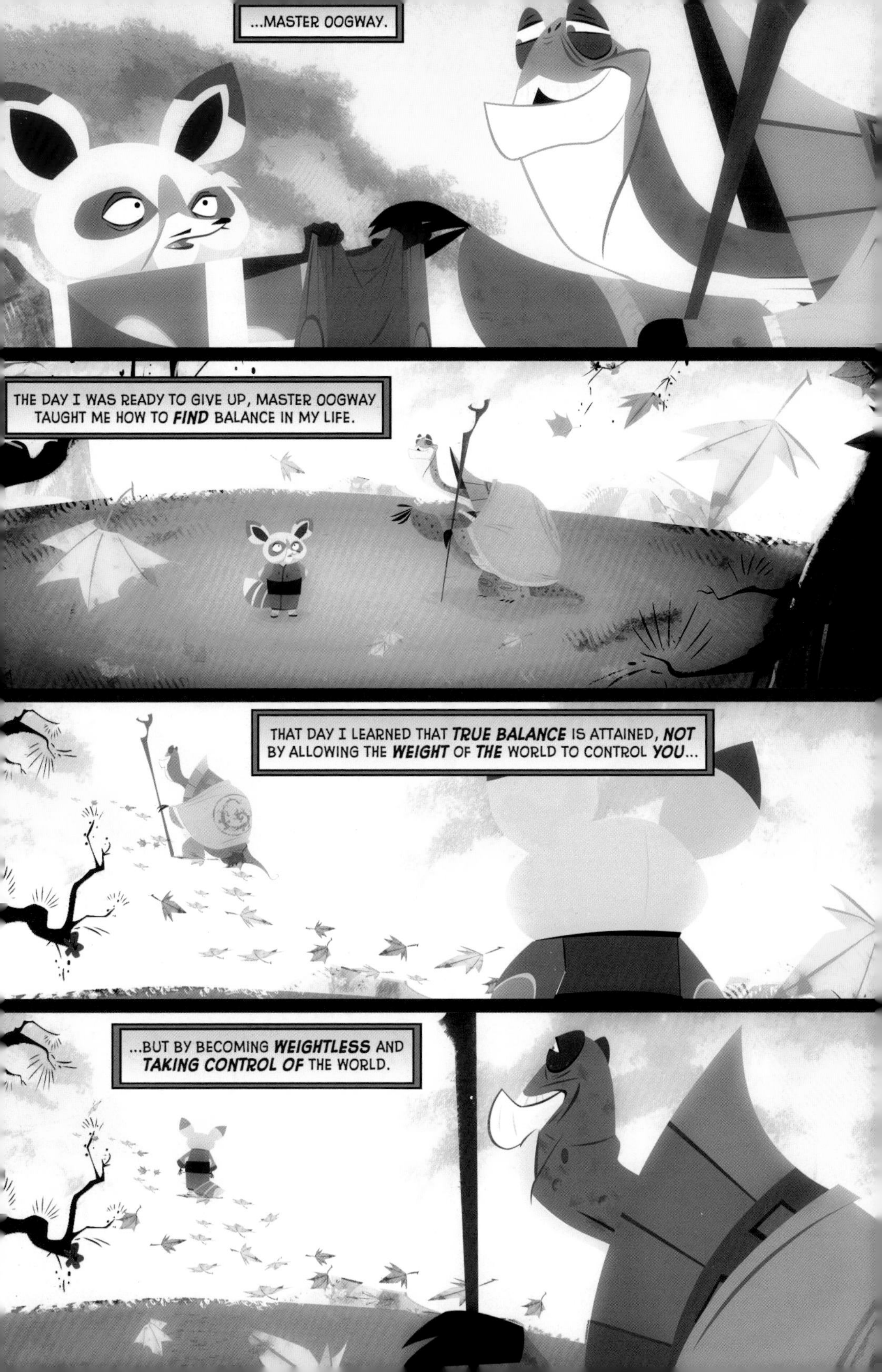
...MASTER OOGWAY.
THE DAY I WAS READY TO GIVE UP, MASTER OOGWAY TAUGHT ME HOW TO **FIND** BALANCE IN MY LIFE.
THAT DAY I LEARNED THAT **TRUE BALANCE** IS ATTAINED, **NOT** BY ALLOWING THE **WEIGHT** OF **THE** WORLD TO CONTROL **YOU**...
...BUT BY BECOMING **WEIGHTLESS** AND **TAKING CONTROL OF** THE WORLD.

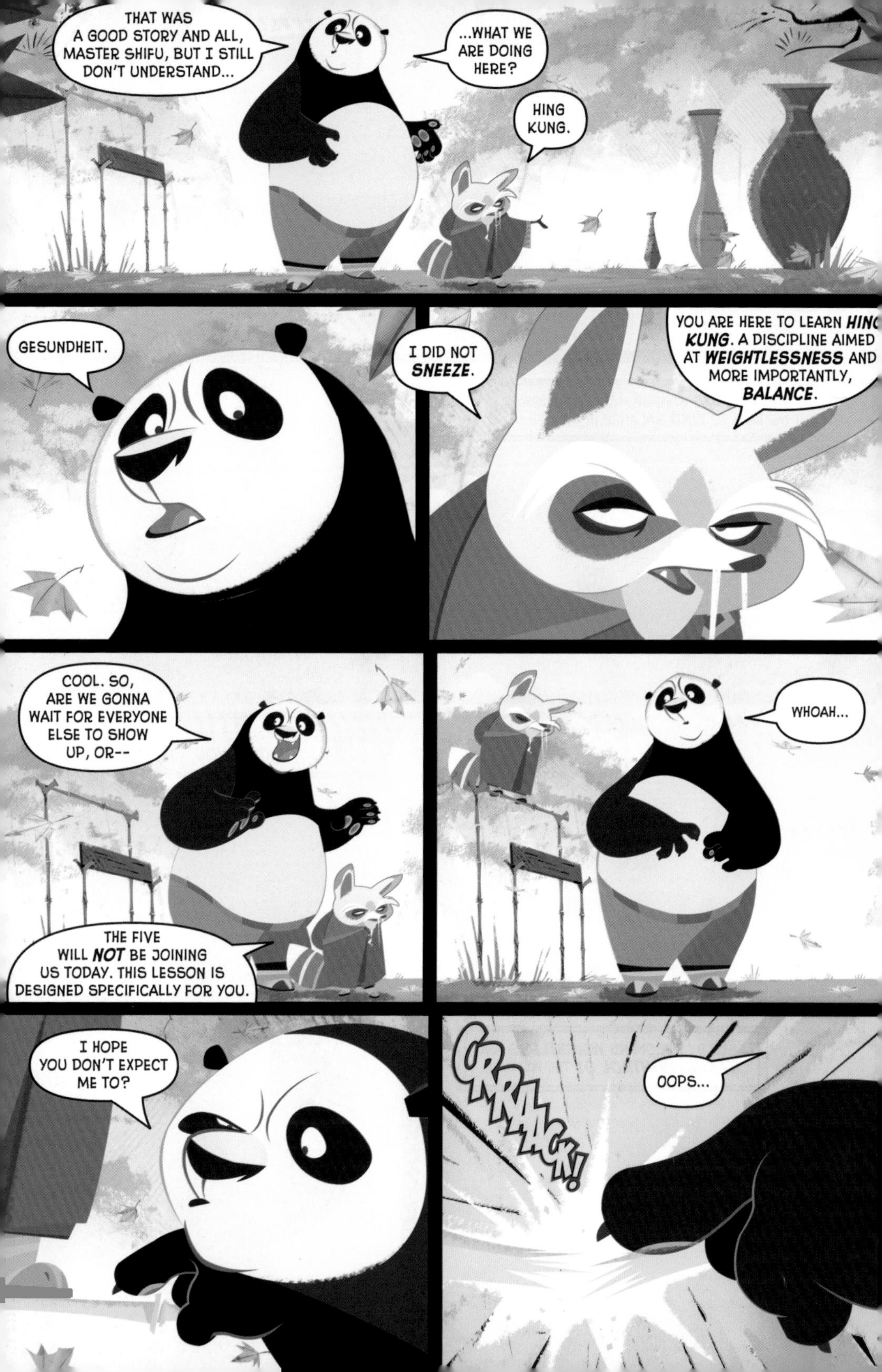
THAT WAS A GOOD STORY AND ALL, MASTER SHIFU, BUT I STILL DON'T UNDERSTAND...
...WHAT WE ARE DOING HERE?
HING KUNG.
GESUNDHEIT.
I DID NOT SNEEZE.
YOU ARE HERE TO LEARN HING KUNG. A DISCIPLINE AIMED AT WEIGHTLESSNESS AND MORE IMPORTANTLY, BALANCE.
COOL. SO, ARE WE GONNA WAIT FOR EVERYONE ELSE TO SHOW UP, OR--
THE FIVE WILL NOT BE JOINING US TODAY. THIS LESSON IS DESIGNED SPECIFICALLY FOR YOU.
WHOAH...
I HOPE YOU DON'T EXPECT ME TO?
CRRAACK!
OOPS...

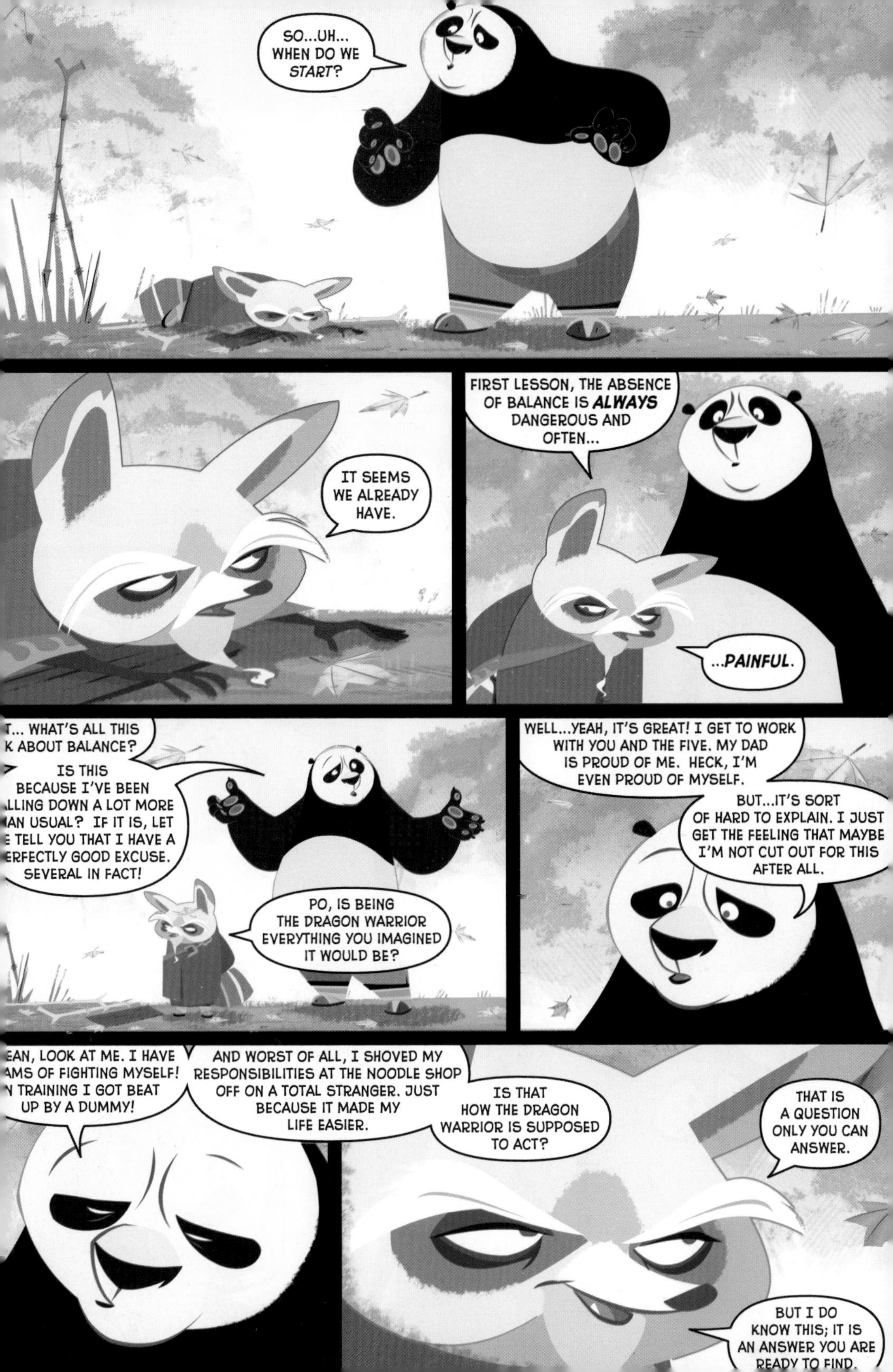
SO...UH... WHEN DO WE START?
IT SEEMS WE ALREADY HAVE.
FIRST LESSON, THE ABSENCE OF BALANCE IS ALWAYS DANGEROUS AND OFTEN...
...PAINFUL.
T... WHAT'S ALL THIS K ABOUT BALANCE?
IS THIS BECAUSE I'VE BEEN LLING DOWN A LOT MORE AN USUAL? IF IT IS, LET E TELL YOU THAT I HAVE A ERFECTLY GOOD EXCUSE. SEVERAL IN FACT!
PO, IS BEING THE DRAGON WARRIOR EVERYTHING YOU IMAGINED IT WOULD BE?
WELL...YEAH, IT'S GREAT! I GET TO WORK WITH YOU AND THE FIVE. MY DAD IS PROUD OF ME. HECK, I'M EVEN PROUD OF MYSELF.
BUT...IT'S SORT OF HARD TO EXPLAIN. I JUST GET THE FEELING THAT MAYBE I'M NOT CUT OUT FOR THIS AFTER ALL.
EAN, LOOK AT ME. I HAVE AMS OF FIGHTING MYSELF! N TRAINING I GOT BEAT UP BY A DUMMY!
AND WORST OF ALL, I SHOVED MY RESPONSIBILITIES AT THE NOODLE SHOP OFF ON A TOTAL STRANGER. JUST BECAUSE IT MADE MY LIFE EASIER.
IS THAT HOW THE DRAGON WARRIOR IS SUPPOSED TO ACT?
THAT IS A QUESTION ONLY YOU CAN ANSWER.
BUT I DO KNOW THIS; IT IS AN ANSWER YOU ARE READY TO FIND.

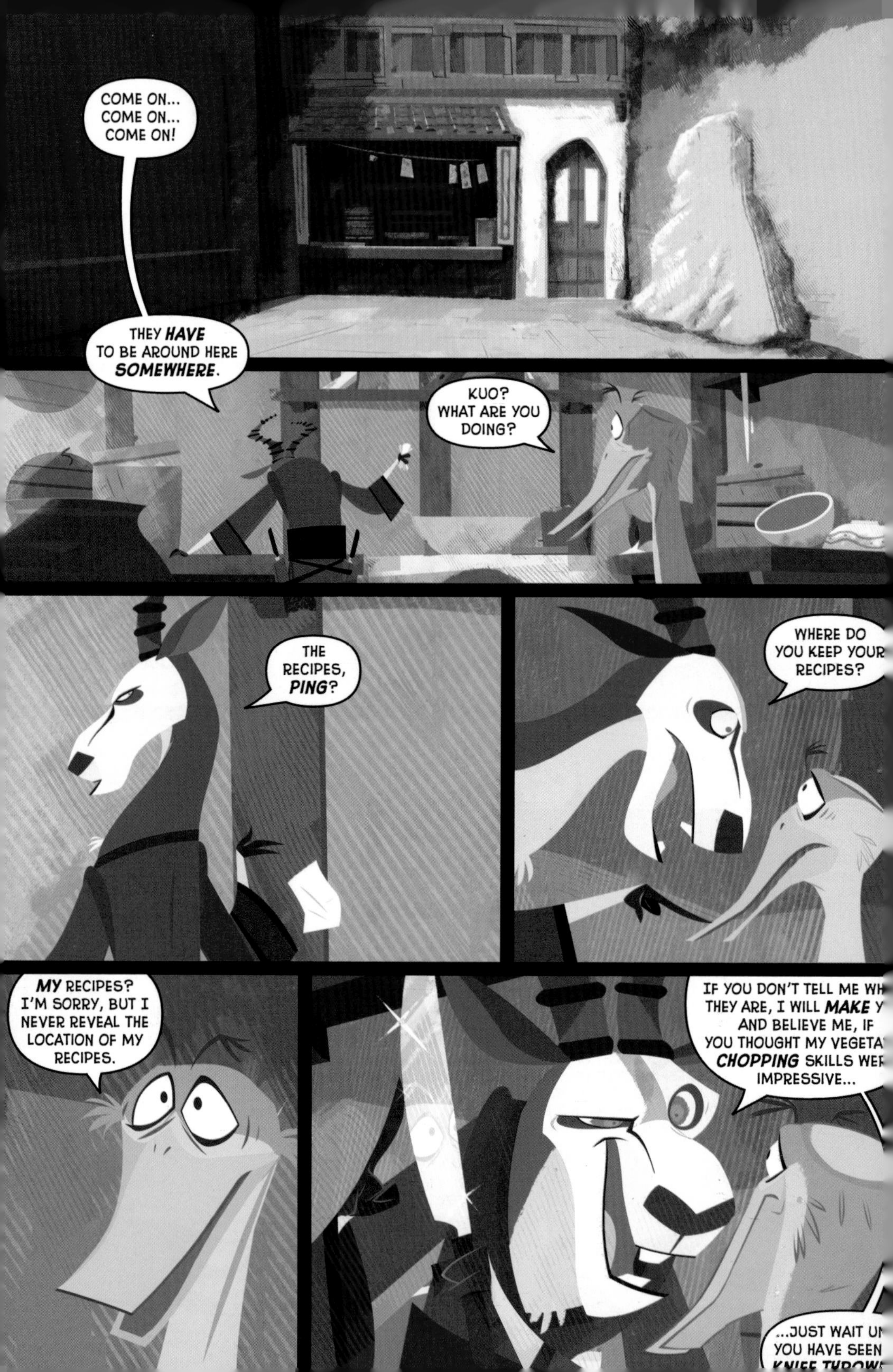
COME ON... COME ON... COME ON!
THEY **HAVE** TO BE AROUND HERE **SOMEWHERE**.
KUO? WHAT ARE YOU DOING?
THE RECIPES, **PING**?
WHERE DO YOU KEEP YOUR RECIPES?
MY RECIPES? I'M SORRY, BUT I NEVER REVEAL THE LOCATION OF MY RECIPES.
IF YOU DON'T TELL ME WH THEY ARE, I WILL **MAKE** Y AND BELIEVE ME, IF YOU THOUGHT MY VEGETA **CHOPPING** SKILLS WER IMPRESSIVE...
...JUST WAIT U YOU HAVE SEEN

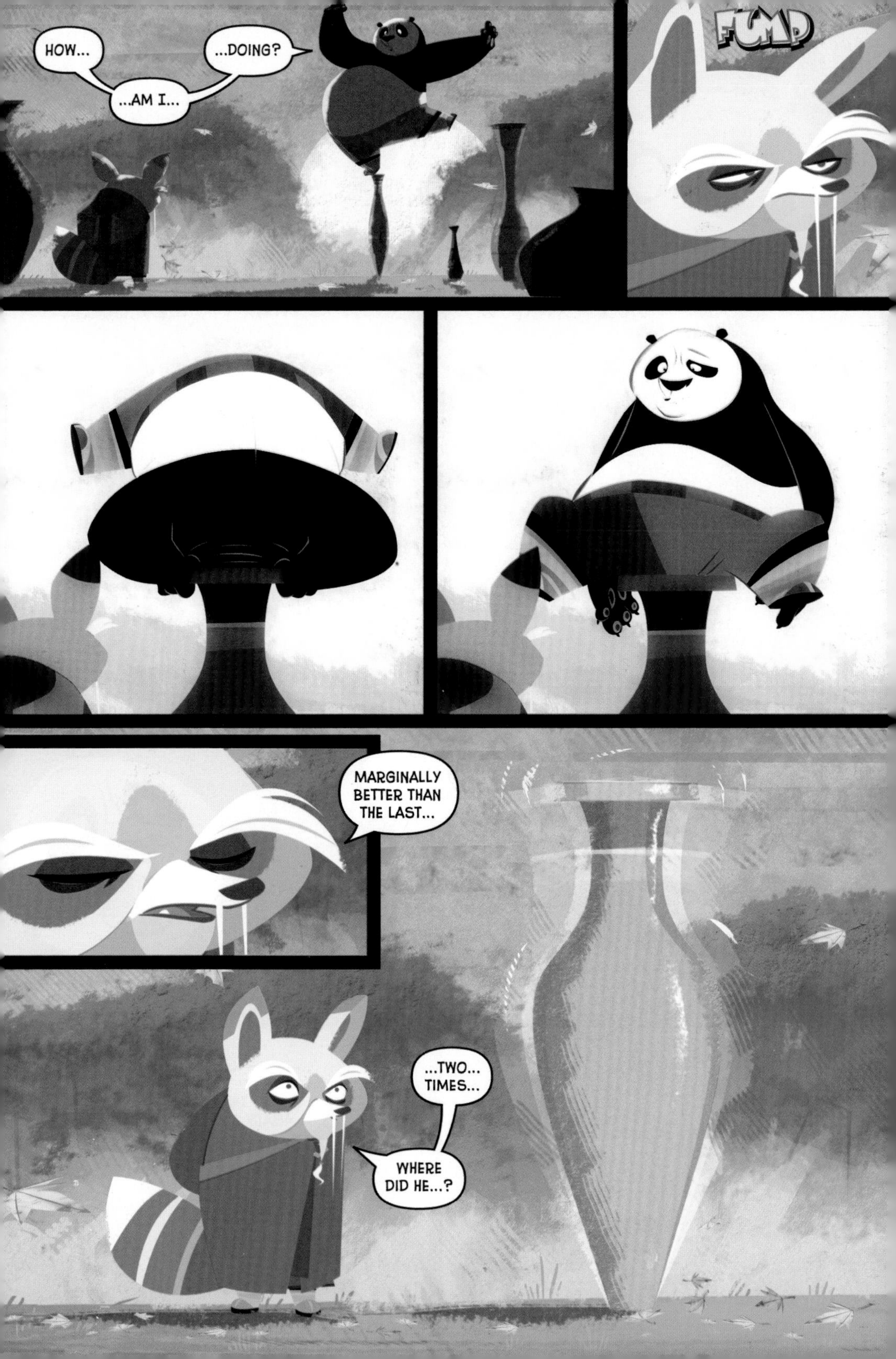
HOW...
...AM I...
...DOING?
FUMP
MARGINALLY BETTER THAN THE LAST...
...TWO... TIMES...
WHERE DID HE...?

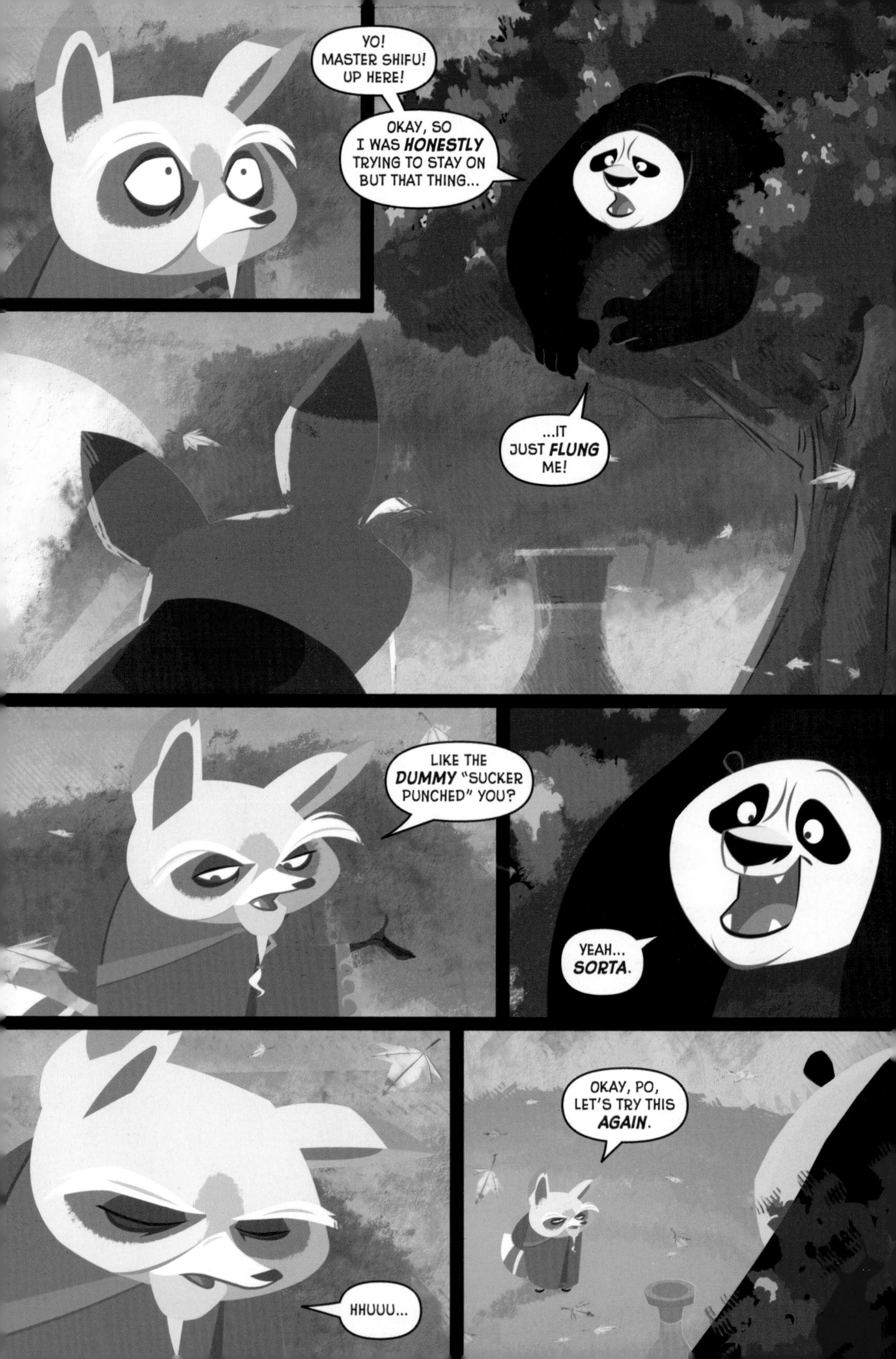
YO! MASTER SHIFU! UP HERE!
OKAY, SO I WAS HONESTLY TRYING TO STAY ON BUT THAT THING...
...IT JUST FLUNG ME!
LIKE THE DUMMY "SUCKER PUNCHED" YOU?
YEAH... SORTA.
HHUUU...
OKAY, PO, LET'S TRY THIS AGAIN.

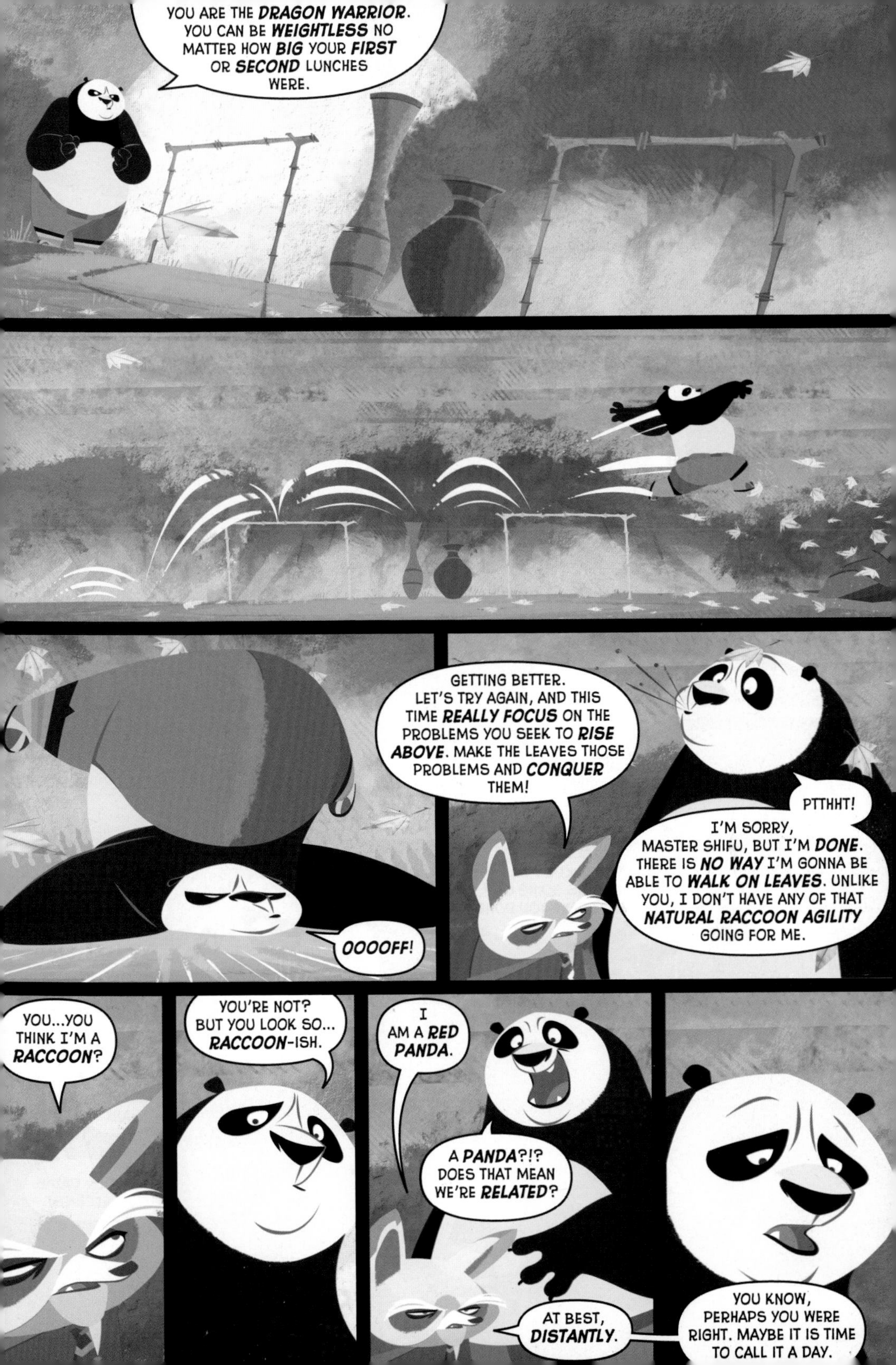
YOU ARE THE DRAGON WARRIOR. YOU CAN BE WEIGHTLESS NO MATTER HOW BIG YOUR FIRST OR SECOND LUNCHES WERE.
OOOOFF!
GETTING BETTER. LET'S TRY AGAIN, AND THIS TIME REALLY FOCUS ON THE PROBLEMS YOU SEEK TO RISE ABOVE. MAKE THE LEAVES THOSE PROBLEMS AND CONQUER THEM!
PTTHHT!
I'M SORRY, MASTER SHIFU, BUT I'M DONE. THERE IS NO WAY I'M GONNA BE ABLE TO WALK ON LEAVES. UNLIKE YOU, I DON'T HAVE ANY OF THAT NATURAL RACCOON AGILITY GOING FOR ME.
YOU...YOU THINK I'M A RACCOON?
YOU'RE NOT? BUT YOU LOOK SO... RACCOON-ISH.
I AM A RED PANDA.
A PANDA?!? DOES THAT MEAN WE'RE RELATED?
AT BEST, DISTANTLY.
YOU KNOW, PERHAPS YOU WERE RIGHT. MAYBE IT IS TIME TO CALL IT A DAY.

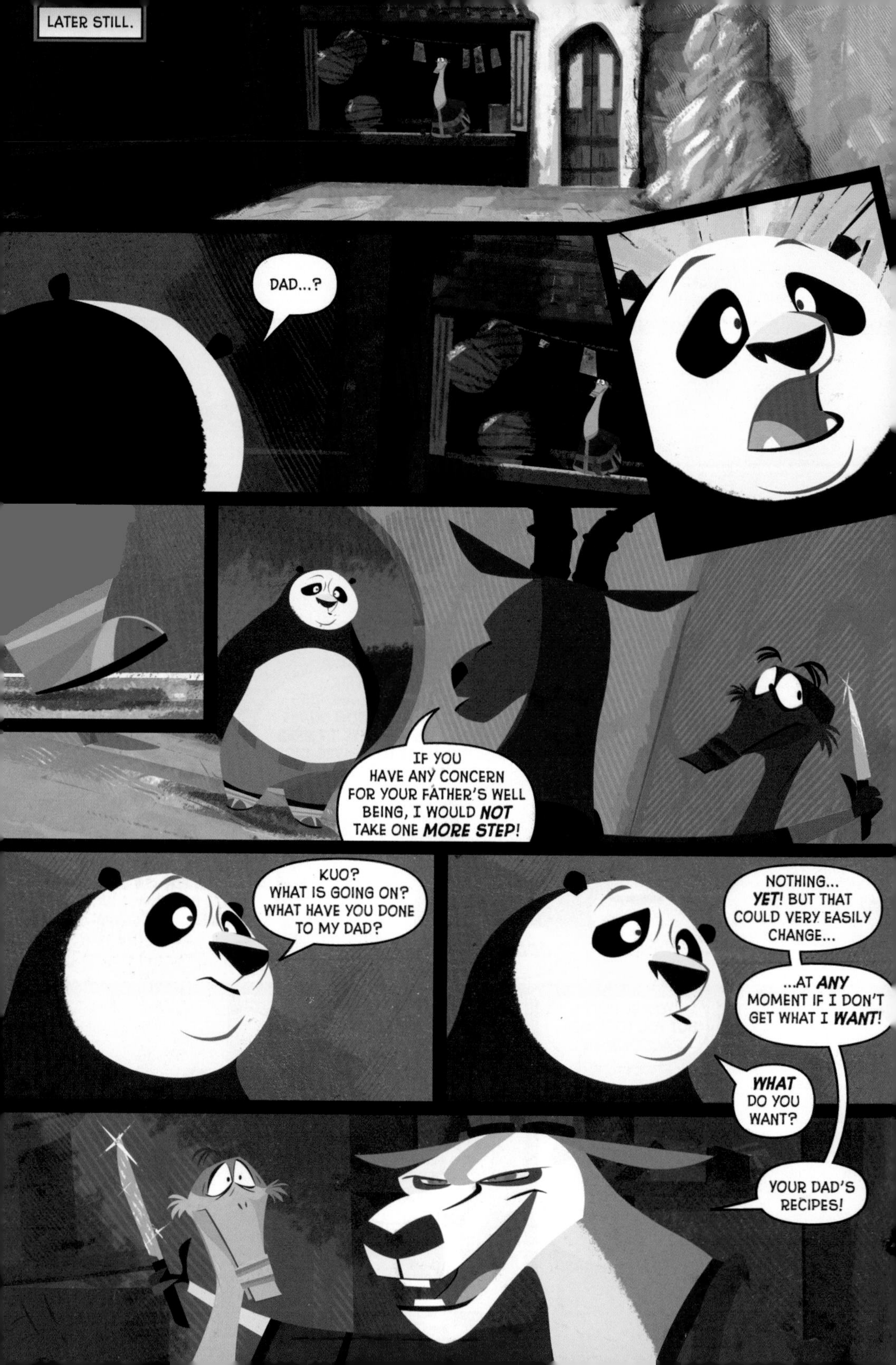
LATER STILL.
DAD...?
IF YOU HAVE ANY CONCERN FOR YOUR FATHER'S WELL BEING, I WOULD *NOT* TAKE ONE *MORE STEP*!
KUO? WHAT IS GOING ON? WHAT HAVE YOU DONE TO MY DAD?
NOTHING... *YET*! BUT THAT COULD VERY EASILY CHANGE...
...AT *ANY* MOMENT IF I DON'T GET WHAT I *WANT*!
WHAT DO YOU WANT?
YOUR DAD'S RECIPES!

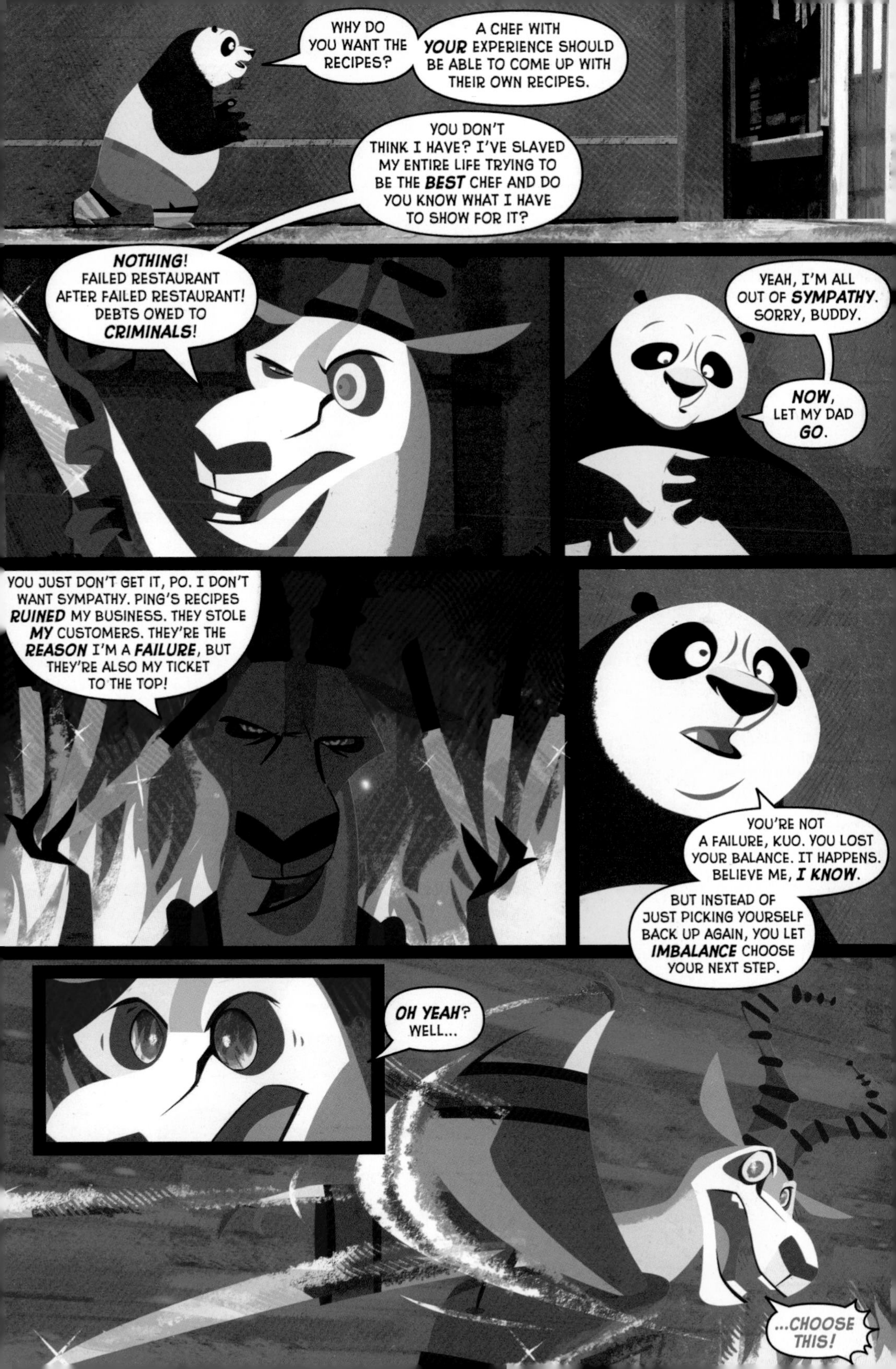
WHY DO YOU WANT THE RECIPES?
A CHEF WITH YOUR EXPERIENCE SHOULD BE ABLE TO COME UP WITH THEIR OWN RECIPES.
YOU DON'T THINK I HAVE? I'VE SLAVED MY ENTIRE LIFE TRYING TO BE THE BEST CHEF AND DO YOU KNOW WHAT I HAVE TO SHOW FOR IT?
NOTHING! FAILED RESTAURANT AFTER FAILED RESTAURANT! DEBTS OWED TO CRIMINALS!
YEAH, I'M ALL OUT OF SYMPATHY. SORRY, BUDDY.
NOW, LET MY DAD GO.
YOU JUST DON'T GET IT, PO. I DON'T WANT SYMPATHY. PING'S RECIPES RUINED MY BUSINESS. THEY STOLE MY CUSTOMERS. THEY'RE THE REASON I'M A FAILURE, BUT THEY'RE ALSO MY TICKET TO THE TOP!
YOU'RE NOT A FAILURE, KUO. YOU LOST YOUR BALANCE. IT HAPPENS. BELIEVE ME, I KNOW.
BUT INSTEAD OF JUST PICKING YOURSELF BACK UP AGAIN, YOU LET IMBALANCE CHOOSE YOUR NEXT STEP.
OH YEAH? WELL...
...CHOOSE THIS!

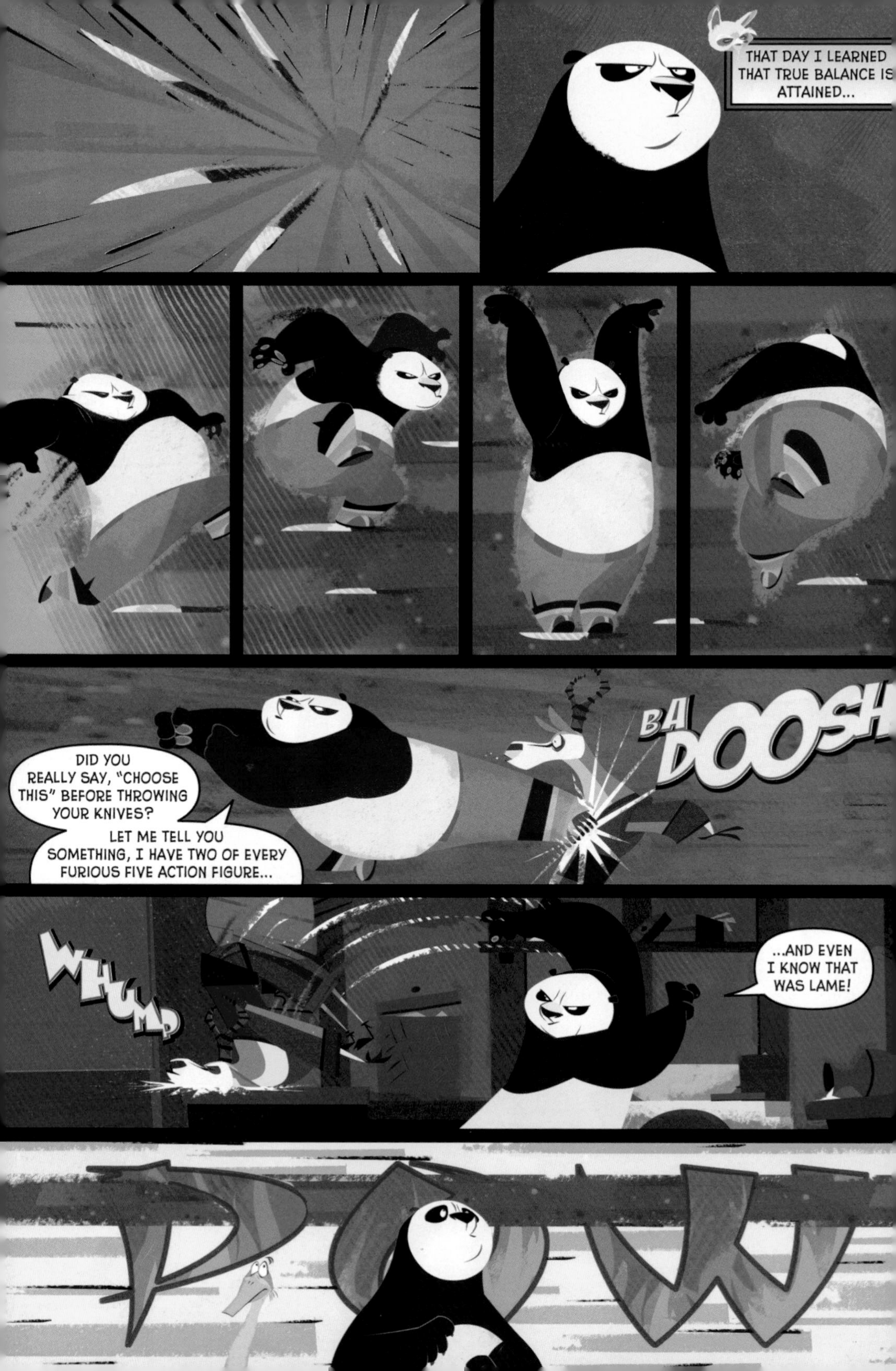
THAT DAY I LEARNED THAT TRUE BALANCE IS ATTAINED...
DID YOU REALLY SAY, "CHOOSE THIS" BEFORE THROWING YOUR KNIVES?
LET ME TELL YOU SOMETHING, I HAVE TWO OF EVERY FURIOUS FIVE ACTION FIGURE...
BA DOOSH
WHUMP
...AND EVEN I KNOW THAT WAS LAME!

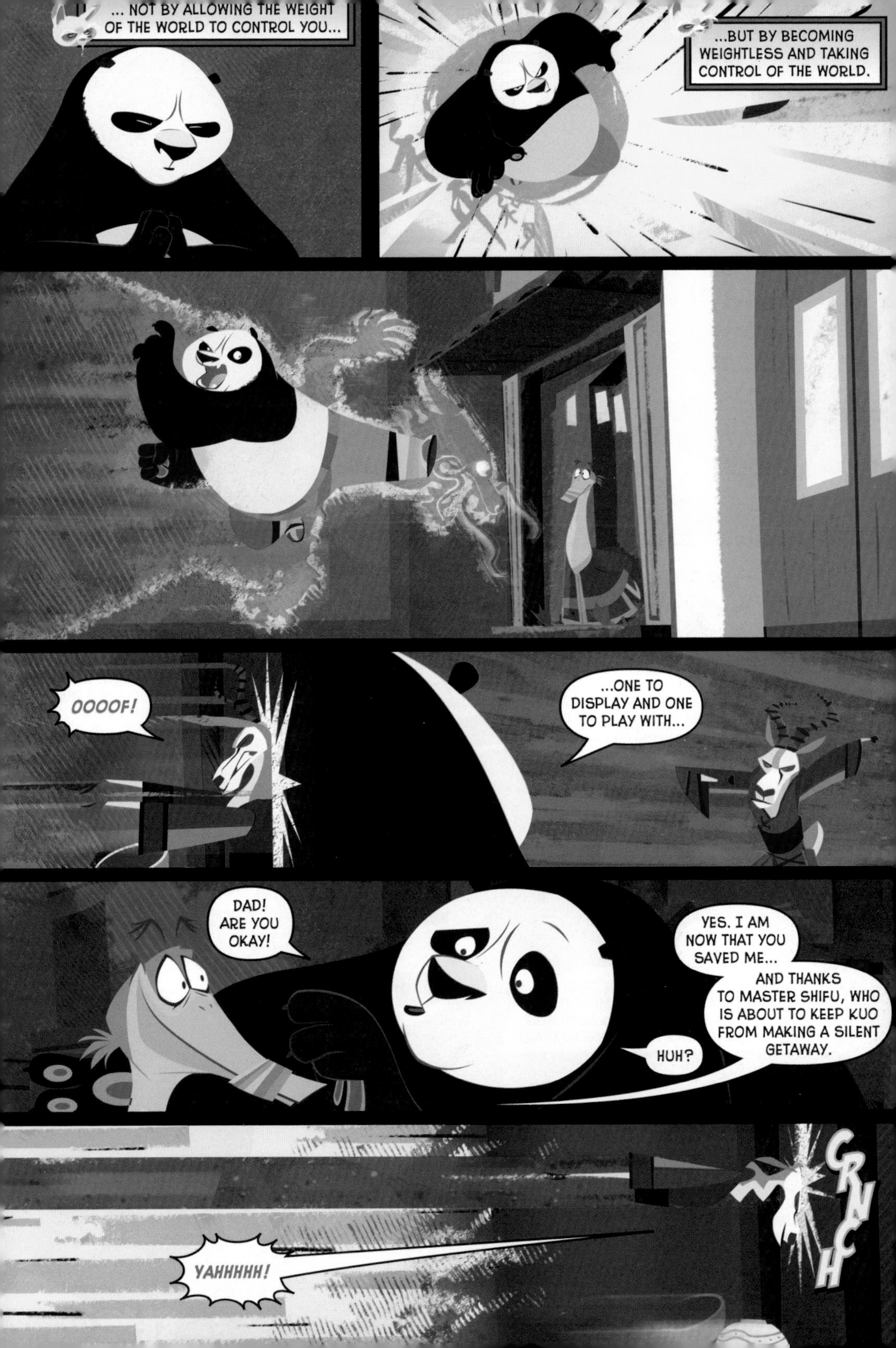
... NOT BY ALLOWING THE WEIGHT OF THE WORLD TO CONTROL YOU...
...BUT BY BECOMING WEIGHTLESS AND TAKING CONTROL OF THE WORLD.
OOOOF!
...ONE TO DISPLAY AND ONE TO PLAY WITH...
DAD! ARE YOU OKAY!
YES. I AM NOW THAT YOU SAVED ME...
AND THANKS TO MASTER SHIFU, WHO IS ABOUT TO KEEP KUO FROM MAKING A SILENT GETAWAY.
HUH?
YAHHHHH!
CRNCH

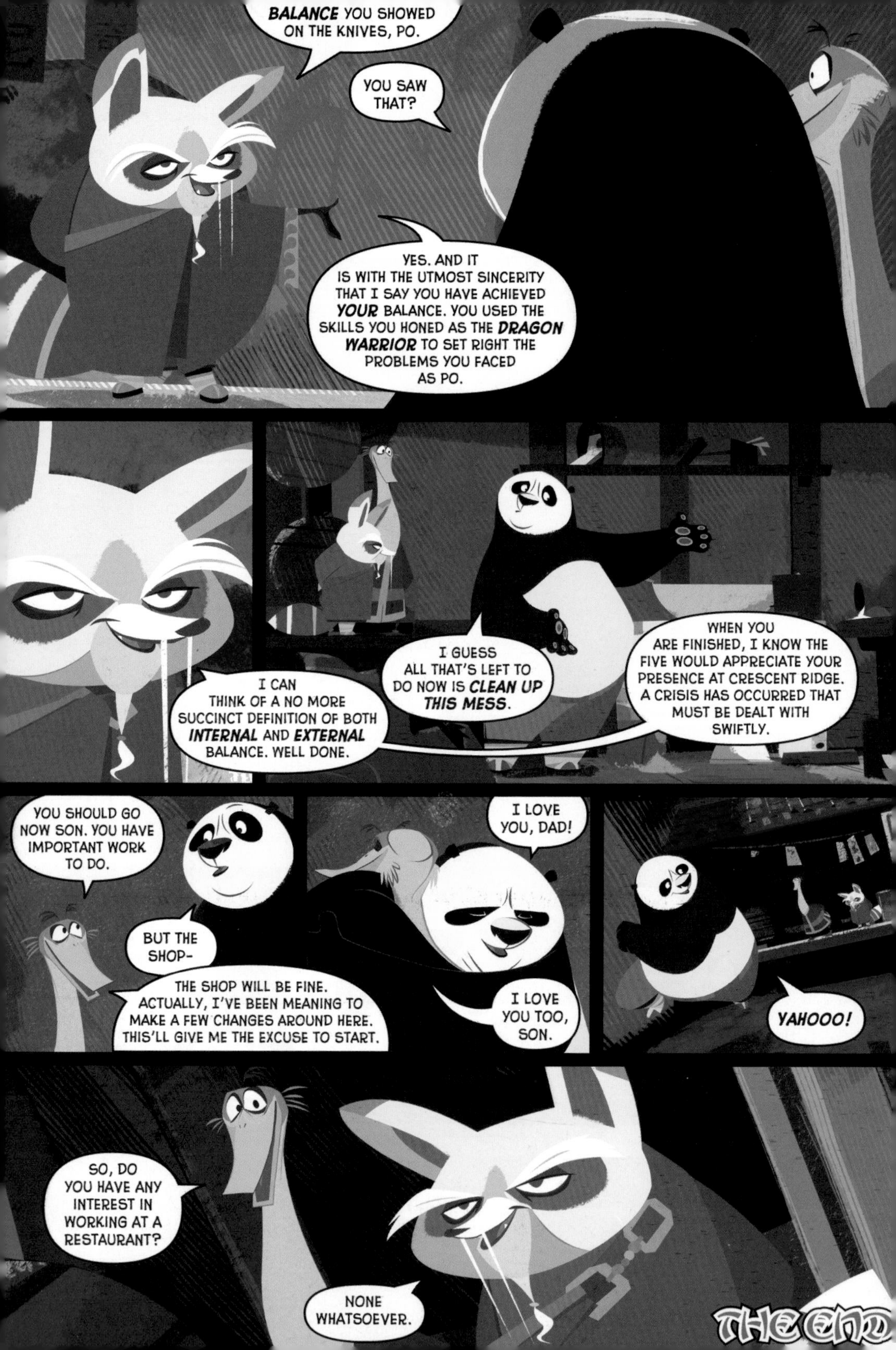
BALANCE YOU SHOWED ON THE KNIVES, PO.
YOU SAW THAT?
YES. AND IT IS WITH THE UTMOST SINCERITY THAT I SAY YOU HAVE ACHIEVED YOUR BALANCE. YOU USED THE SKILLS YOU HONED AS THE DRAGON WARRIOR TO SET RIGHT THE PROBLEMS YOU FACED AS PO.
I CAN THINK OF A NO MORE SUCCINCT DEFINITION OF BOTH INTERNAL AND EXTERNAL BALANCE. WELL DONE.
I GUESS ALL THAT'S LEFT TO DO NOW IS CLEAN UP THIS MESS.
WHEN YOU ARE FINISHED, I KNOW THE FIVE WOULD APPRECIATE YOUR PRESENCE AT CRESCENT RIDGE. A CRISIS HAS OCCURRED THAT MUST BE DEALT WITH SWIFTLY.
YOU SHOULD GO NOW SON. YOU HAVE IMPORTANT WORK TO DO.
BUT THE SHOP-
THE SHOP WILL BE FINE. ACTUALLY, I'VE BEEN MEANING TO MAKE A FEW CHANGES AROUND HERE. THIS'LL GIVE ME THE EXCUSE TO START.
I LOVE YOU, DAD!
I LOVE YOU TOO, SON.
YAHOOO!
SO, DO YOU HAVE ANY INTEREST IN WORKING AT A RESTAURANT?
NONE WHATSOEVER.
THE END

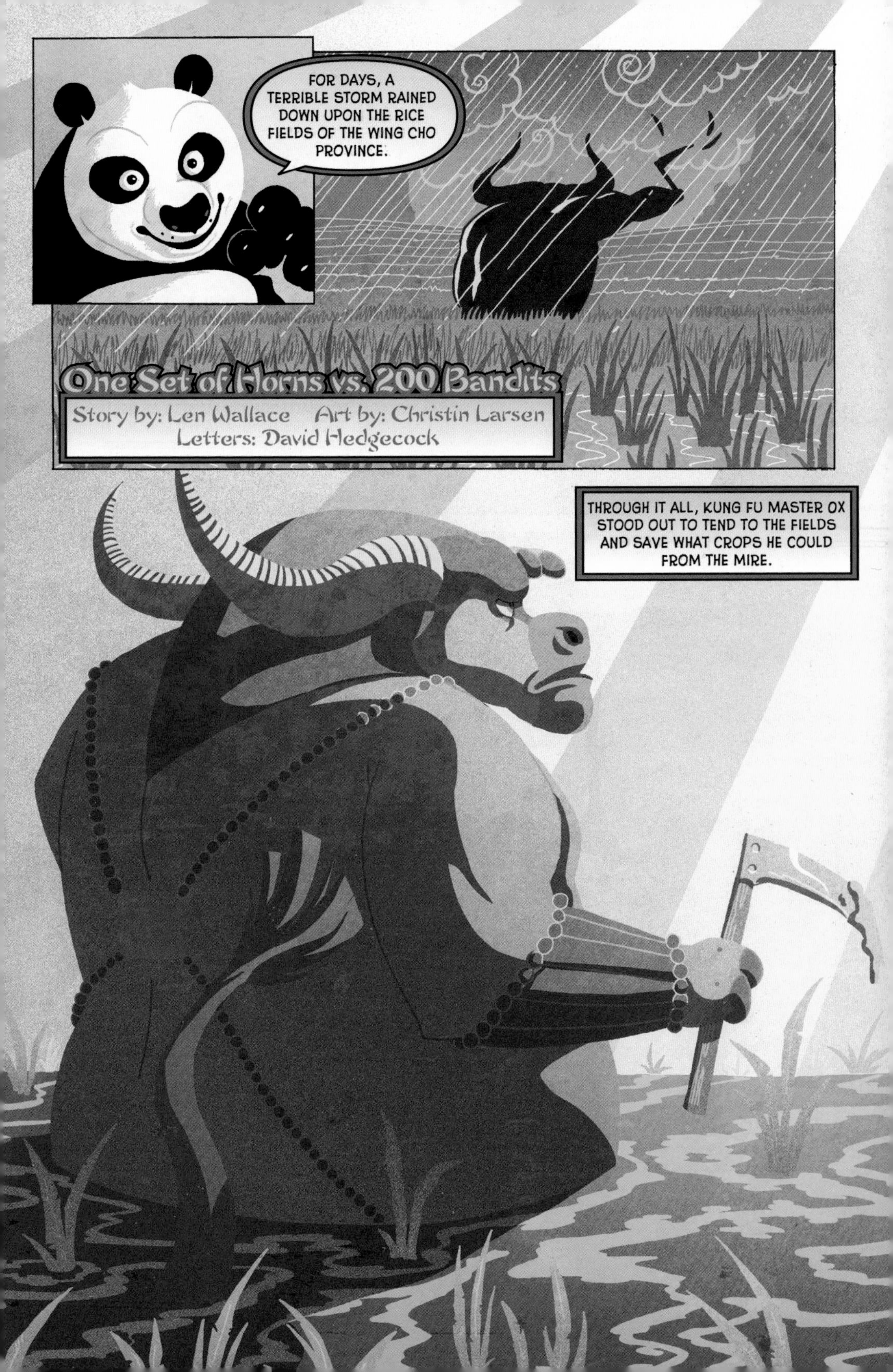
FOR DAYS, A TERRIBLE STORM RAINED DOWN UPON THE RICE FIELDS OF THE WING CHO PROVINCE.
One Set of Horns vs. 200 Bandits
Story by: Len Wallace Art by: Christin Larsen
Letters: David Hedgecock
THROUGH IT ALL, KUNG FU MASTER OX STOOD OUT TO TEND TO THE FIELDS AND SAVE WHAT CROPS HE COULD FROM THE MIRE.

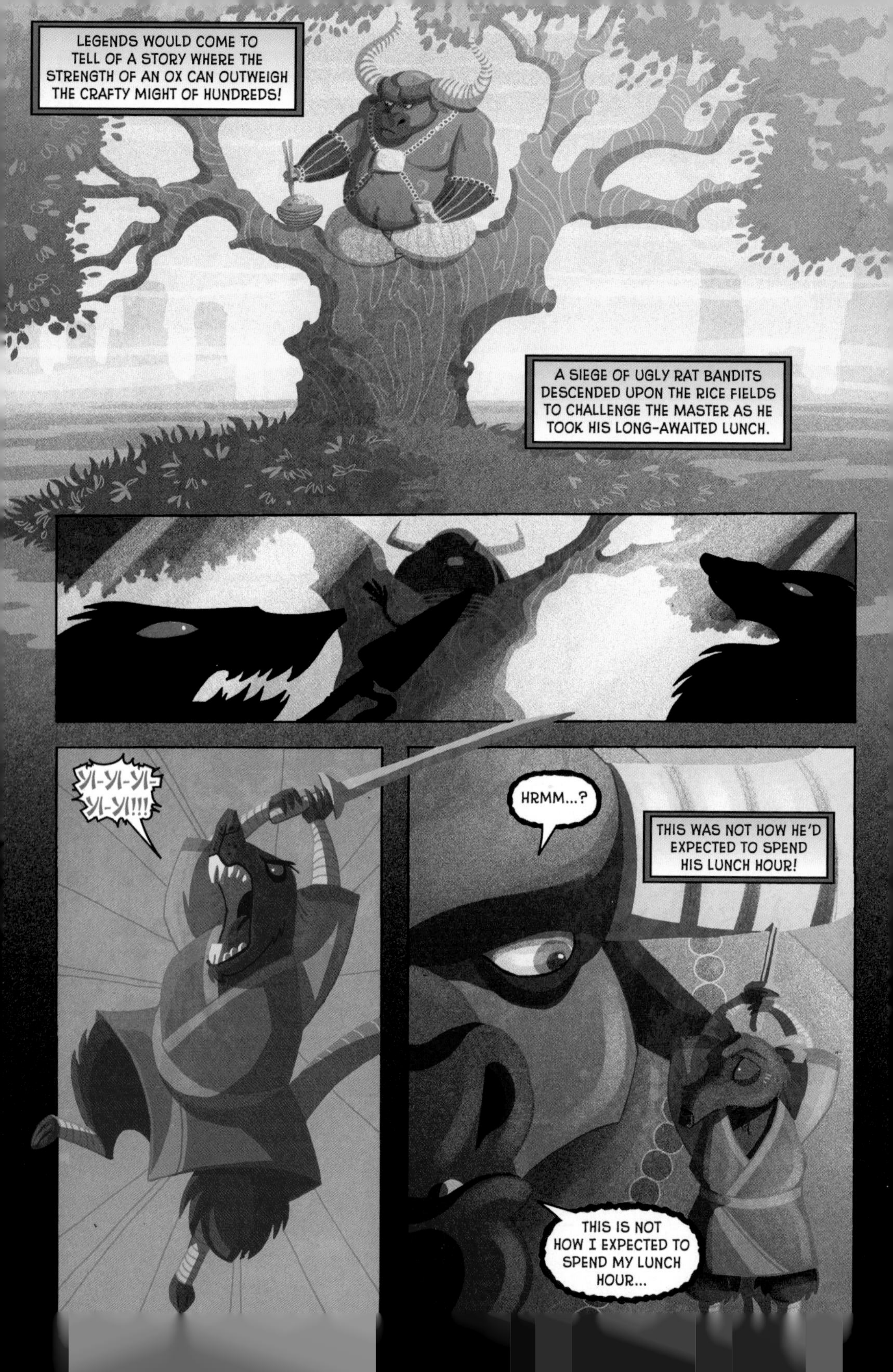
LEGENDS WOULD COME TO TELL OF A STORY WHERE THE STRENGTH OF AN OX CAN OUTWEIGH THE CRAFTY MIGHT OF HUNDREDS!
A SIEGE OF UGLY RAT BANDITS DESCENDED UPON THE RICE FIELDS TO CHALLENGE THE MASTER AS HE TOOK HIS LONG-AWAITED LUNCH.
YI-YI-YI-YI-YI!!!
HRMM...?
THIS WAS NOT HOW HE'D EXPECTED TO SPEND HIS LUNCH HOUR!
THIS IS NOT HOW I EXPECTED TO SPEND MY LUNCH HOUR...

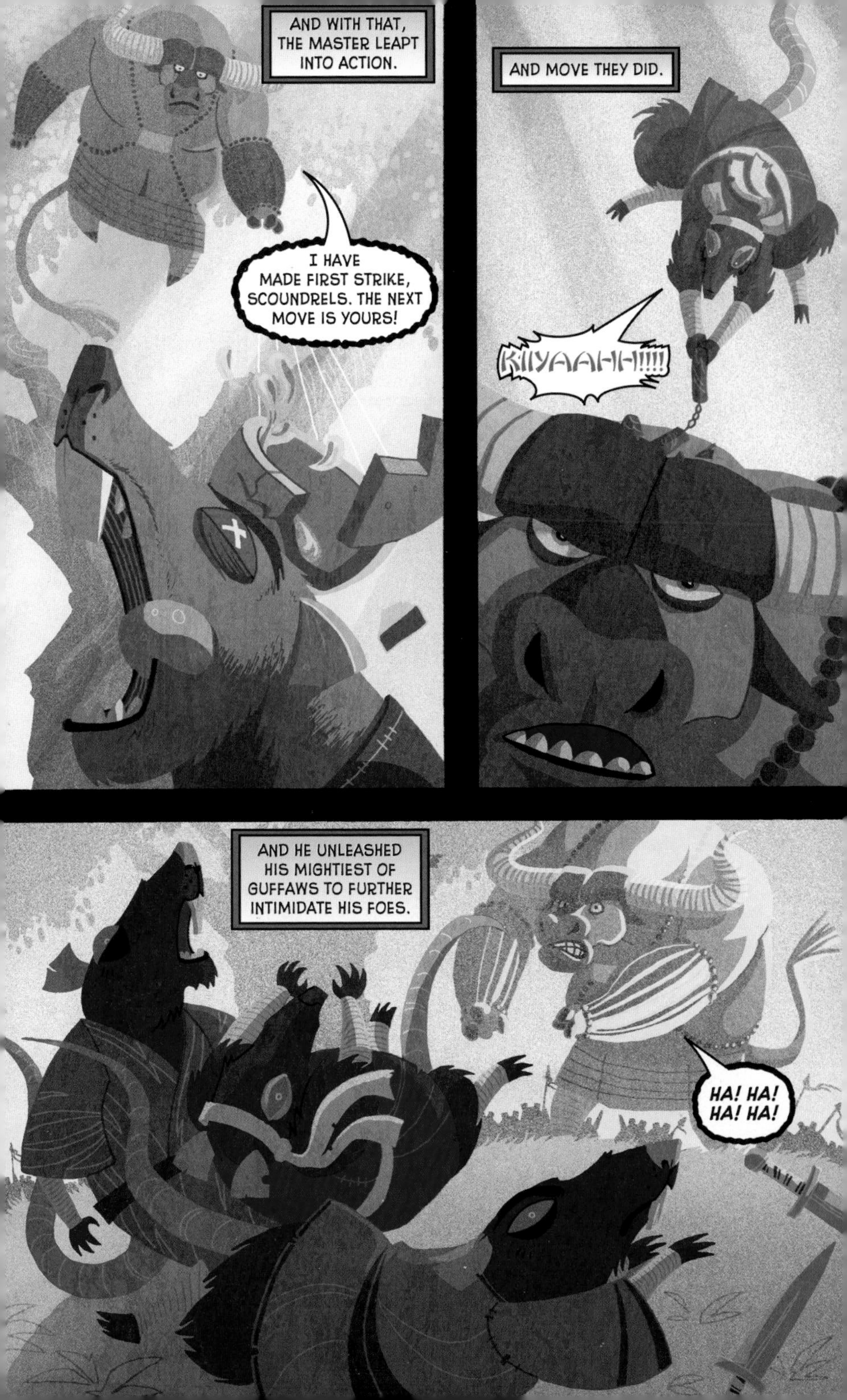
AND WITH THAT, THE MASTER LEAPT INTO ACTION.
I HAVE MADE FIRST STRIKE, SCOUNDRELS. THE NEXT MOVE IS YOURS!
AND MOVE THEY DID.
KIIYAAHH!!!!
AND HE UNLEASHED HIS MIGHTIEST OF GUFFAWS TO FURTHER INTIMIDATE HIS FOES.
HA! HA! HA! HA!

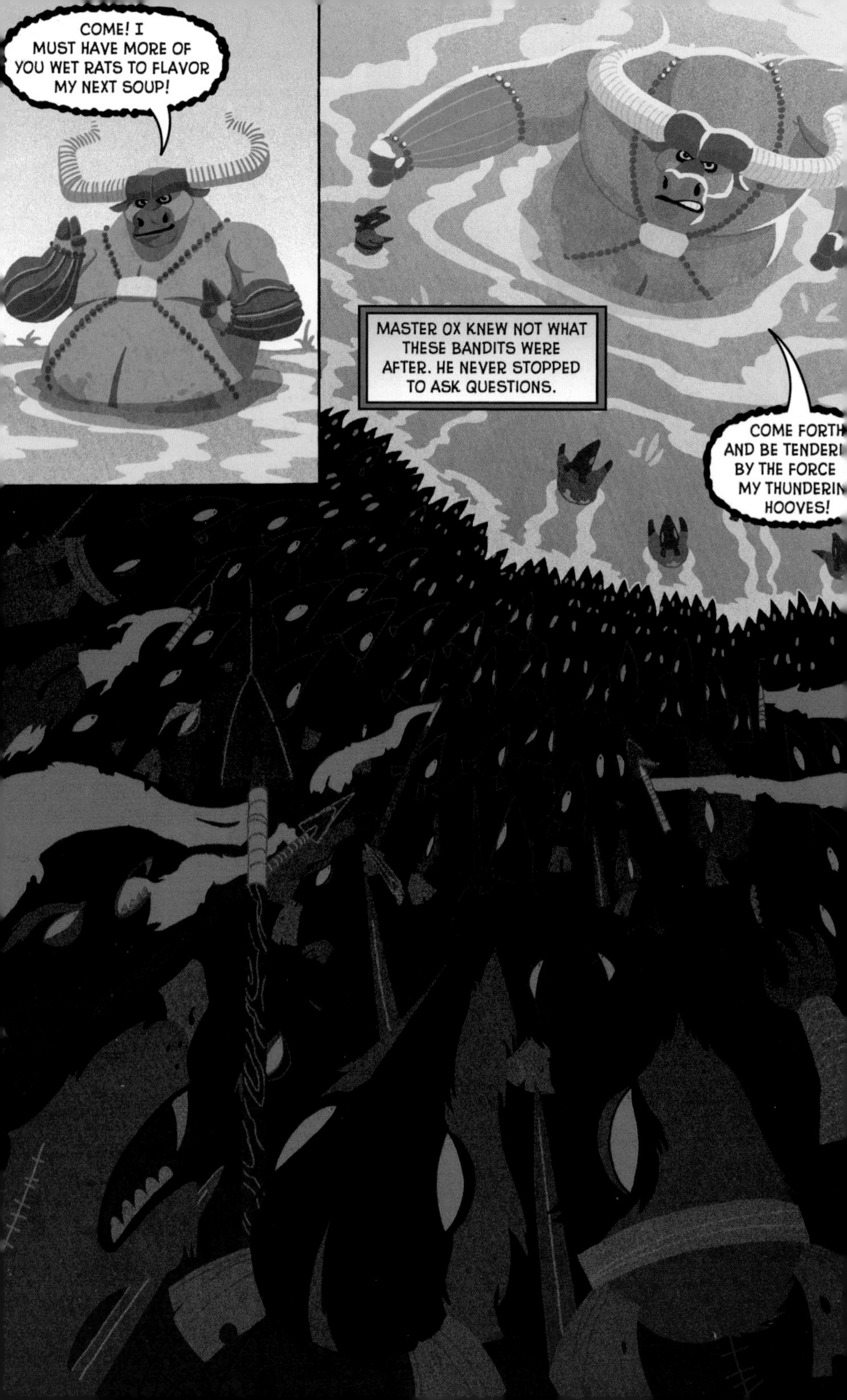
COME! I MUST HAVE MORE OF YOU WET RATS TO FLAVOR MY NEXT SOUP!
MASTER OX KNEW NOT WHAT THESE BANDITS WERE AFTER. HE NEVER STOPPED TO ASK QUESTIONS.
COME FORTH AND BE TENDERI BY THE FORCE MY THUNDERIN HOOVES!

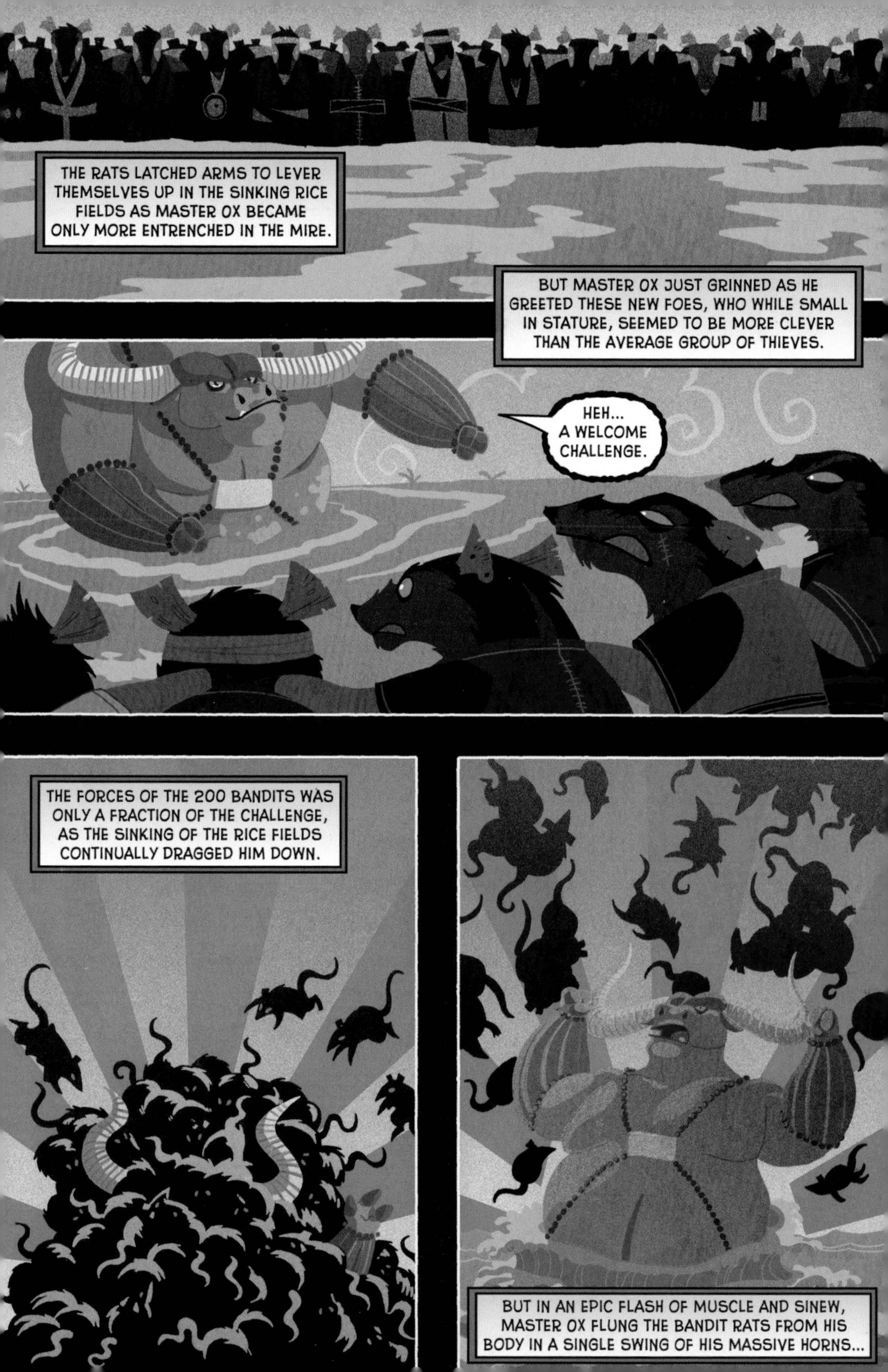
THE RATS LATCHED ARMS TO LEVER THEMSELVES UP IN THE SINKING RICE FIELDS AS MASTER OX BECAME ONLY MORE ENTRENCHED IN THE MIRE.
BUT MASTER OX JUST GRINNED AS HE GREETED THESE NEW FOES, WHO WHILE SMALL IN STATURE, SEEMED TO BE MORE CLEVER THAN THE AVERAGE GROUP OF THIEVES.
HEH... A WELCOME CHALLENGE.
THE FORCES OF THE 200 BANDITS WAS ONLY A FRACTION OF THE CHALLENGE, AS THE SINKING OF THE RICE FIELDS CONTINUALLY DRAGGED HIM DOWN.
BUT IN AN EPIC FLASH OF MUSCLE AND SINEW, MASTER OX FLUNG THE BANDIT RATS FROM HIS BODY IN A SINGLE SWING OF HIS MASSIVE HORNS...

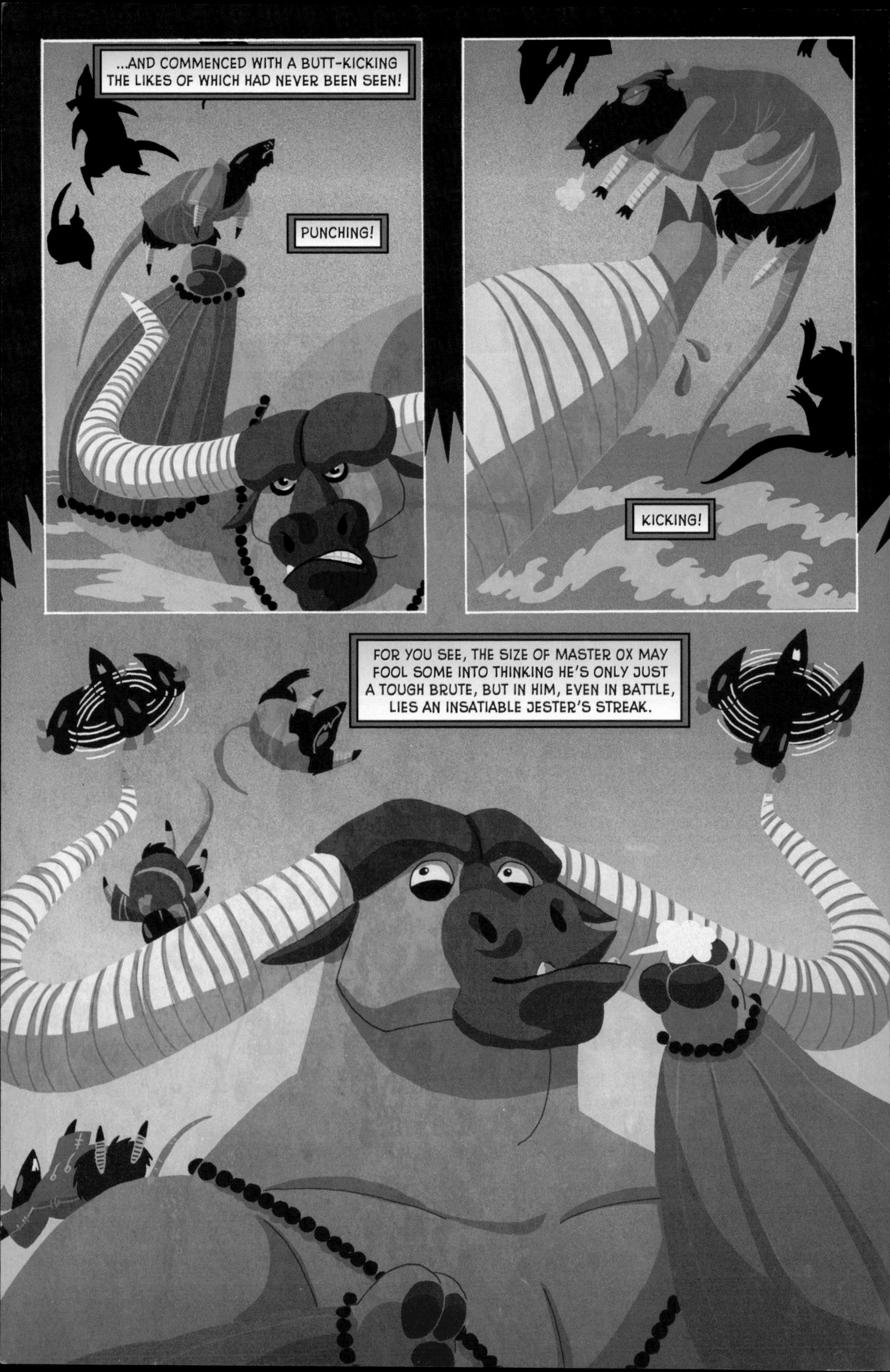
...AND COMMENCED WITH A BUTT-KICKING THE LIKES OF WHICH HAD NEVER BEEN SEEN!
PUNCHING!
KICKING!
FOR YOU SEE, THE SIZE OF MASTER OX MAY FOOL SOME INTO THINKING HE'S ONLY JUST A TOUGH BRUTE, BUT IN HIM, EVEN IN BATTLE, LIES AN INSATIABLE JESTER'S STREAK.

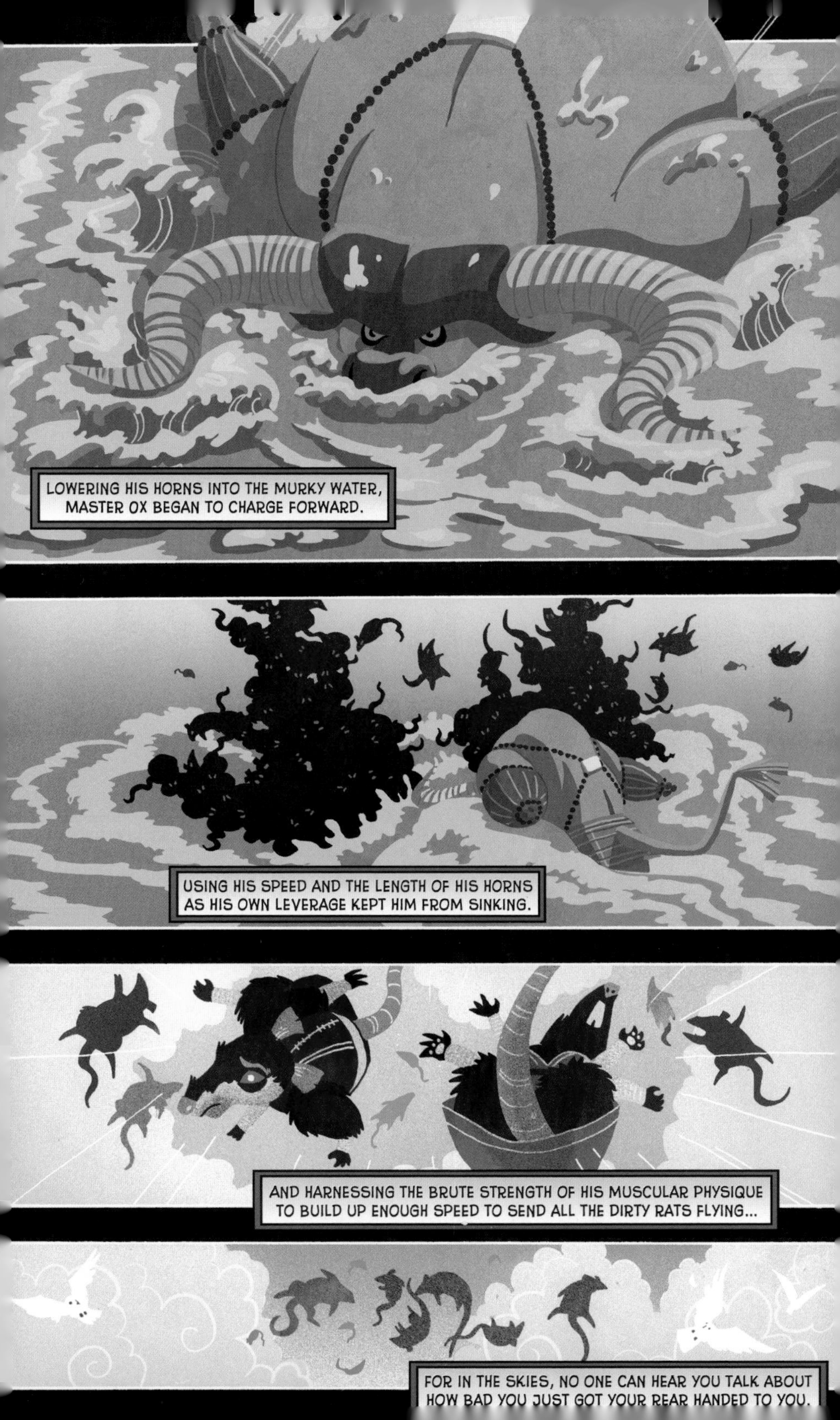
LOWERING HIS HORNS INTO THE MURKY WATER, MASTER OX BEGAN TO CHARGE FORWARD.
USING HIS SPEED AND THE LENGTH OF HIS HORNS AS HIS OWN LEVERAGE KEPT HIM FROM SINKING.
AND HARNESSING THE BRUTE STRENGTH OF HIS MUSCULAR PHYSIQUE TO BUILD UP ENOUGH SPEED TO SEND ALL THE DIRTY RATS FLYING...
FOR IN THE SKIES, NO ONE CAN HEAR YOU TALK ABOUT HOW BAD YOU JUST GOT YOUR REAR HANDED TO YOU.

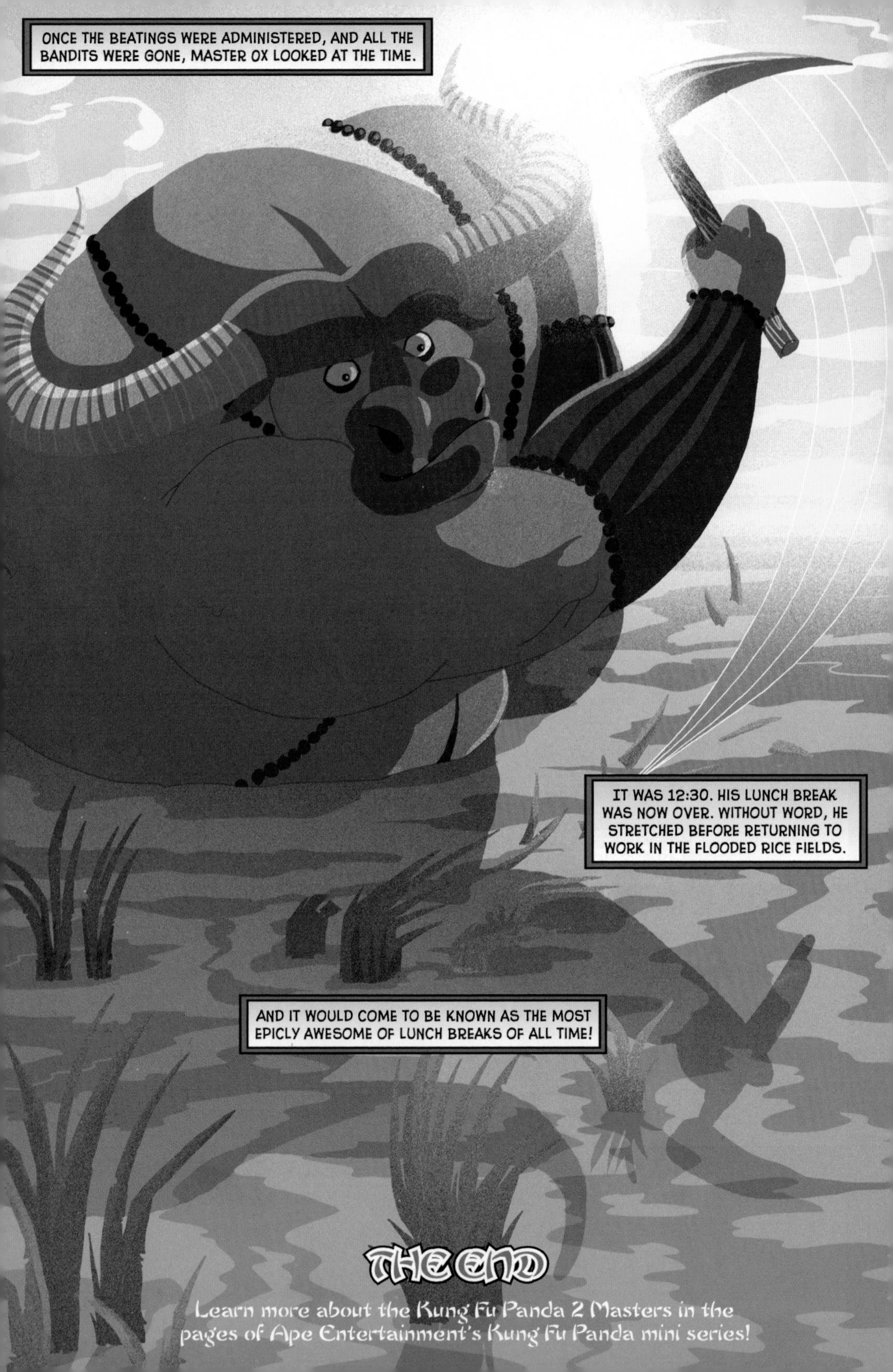
ONCE THE BEATINGS WERE ADMINISTERED, AND ALL THE BANDITS WERE GONE, MASTER OX LOOKED AT THE TIME.
IT WAS 12:30. HIS LUNCH BREAK WAS NOW OVER. WITHOUT WORD, HE STRETCHED BEFORE RETURNING TO WORK IN THE FLOODED RICE FIELDS.
AND IT WOULD COME TO BE KNOWN AS THE MOST EPICLY AWESOME OF LUNCH BREAKS OF ALL TIME!
THE END
Learn more about the Kung Fu Panda 2 Masters in the pages of Ape Entertainment's Kung Fu Panda mini series!

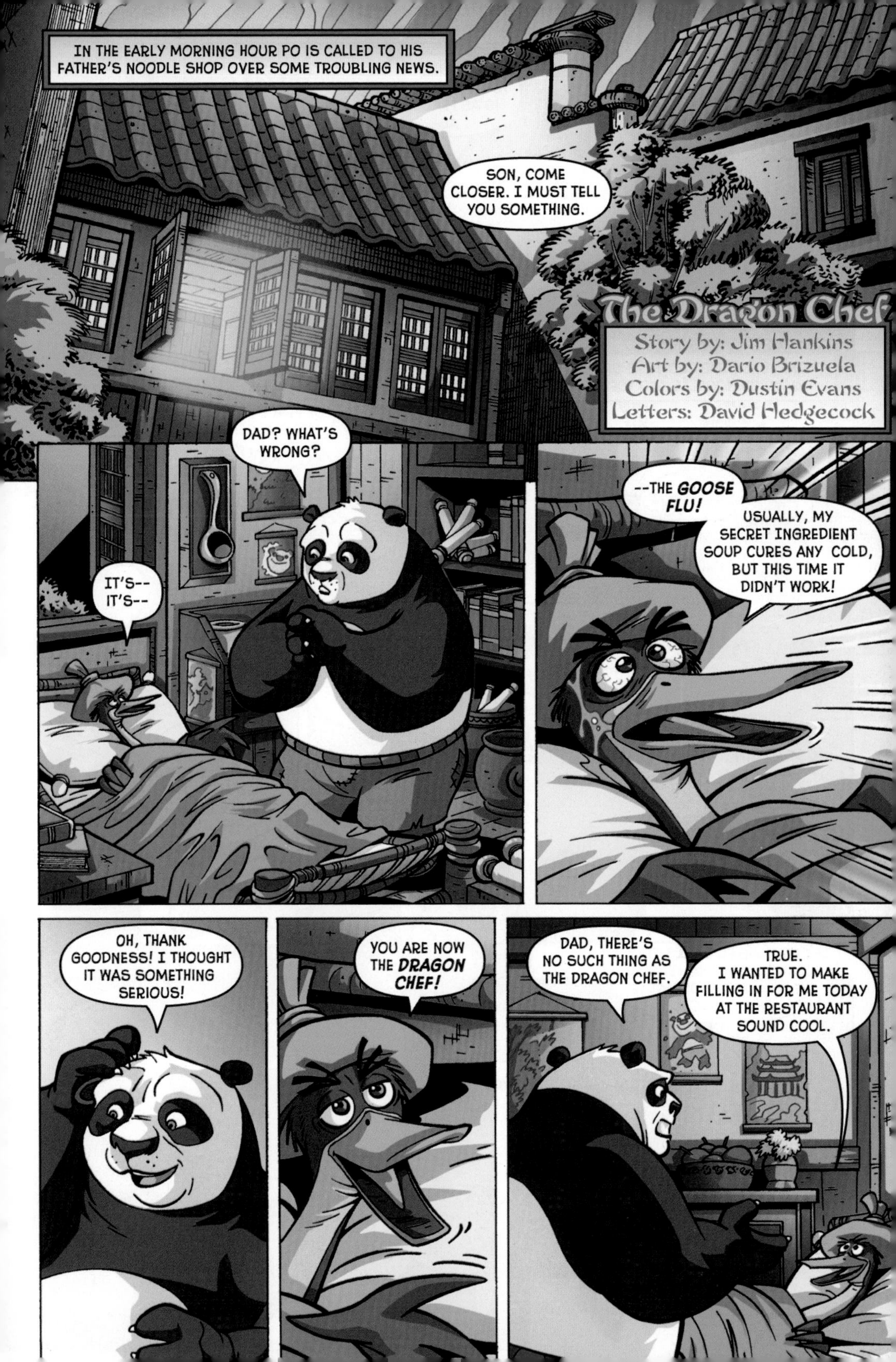
IN THE EARLY MORNING HOUR PO IS CALLED TO HIS FATHER'S NOODLE SHOP OVER SOME TROUBLING NEWS.
SON, COME CLOSER. I MUST TELL YOU SOMETHING.
The Dragon Chef
Story by: Jim Hankins
Art by: Dario Brizuela
Colors by: Dustin Evans
Letters: David Hedgecock
DAD? WHAT'S WRONG?
IT'S-- IT'S--
--THE GOOSE FLU!
USUALLY, MY SECRET INGREDIENT SOUP CURES ANY COLD, BUT THIS TIME IT DIDN'T WORK!
OH, THANK GOODNESS! I THOUGHT IT WAS SOMETHING SERIOUS!
YOU ARE NOW THE DRAGON CHEF!
DAD, THERE'S NO SUCH THING AS THE DRAGON CHEF.
TRUE. I WANTED TO MAKE FILLING IN FOR ME TODAY AT THE RESTAURANT SOUND COOL.

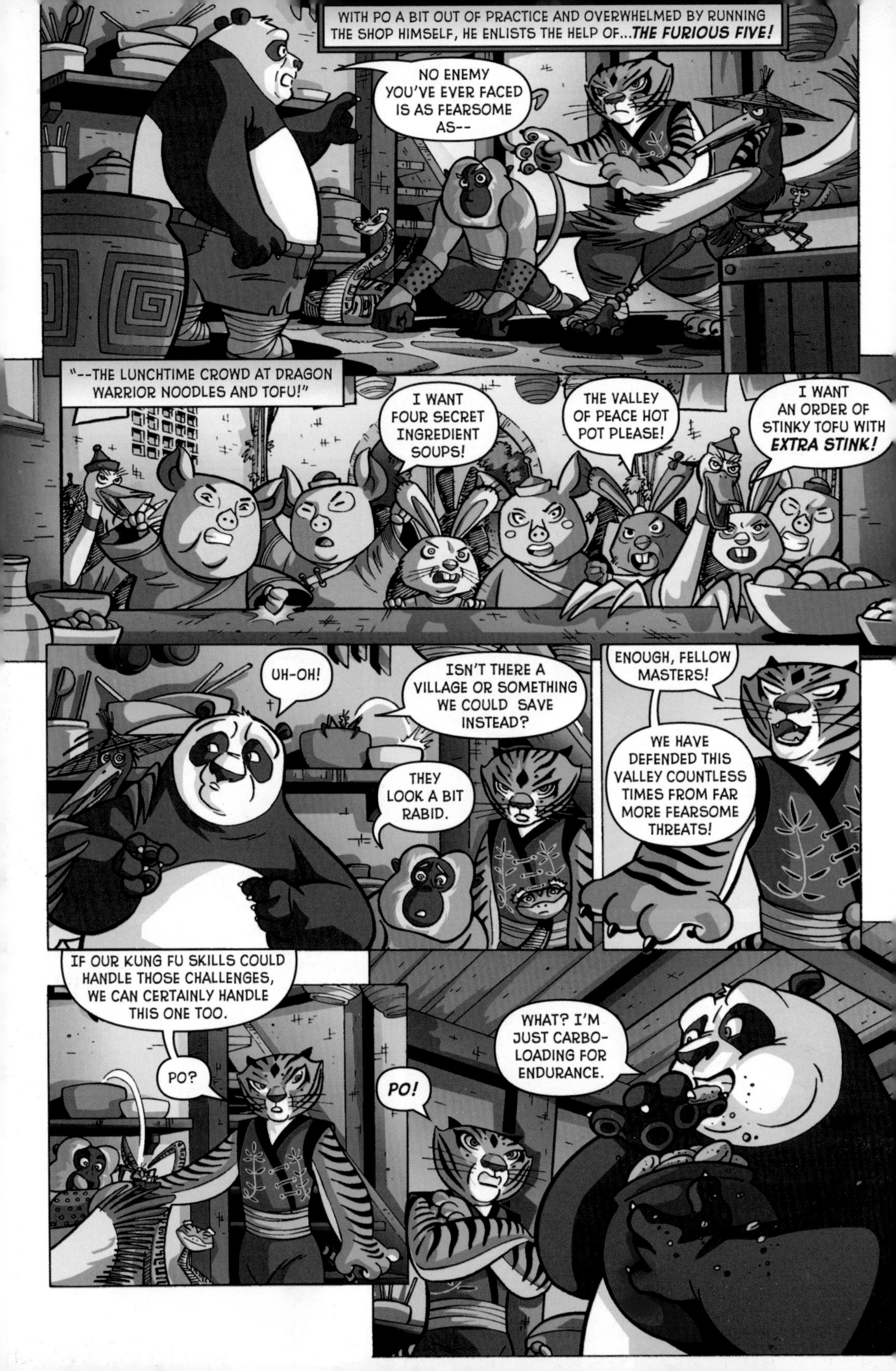
WITH PO A BIT OUT OF PRACTICE AND OVERWHELMED BY RUNNING THE SHOP HIMSELF, HE ENLISTS THE HELP OF... THE FURIOUS FIVE!
NO ENEMY YOU'VE EVER FACED IS AS FEARSOME AS--
"--THE LUNCHTIME CROWD AT DRAGON WARRIOR NOODLES AND TOFU!"
I WANT FOUR SECRET INGREDIENT SOUPS!
THE VALLEY OF PEACE HOT POT PLEASE!
I WANT AN ORDER OF STINKY TOFU WITH EXTRA STINK!
UH-OH!
ISN'T THERE A VILLAGE OR SOMETHING WE COULD SAVE INSTEAD?
THEY LOOK A BIT RABID.
ENOUGH, FELLOW MASTERS!
WE HAVE DEFENDED THIS VALLEY COUNTLESS TIMES FROM FAR MORE FEARSOME THREATS!
IF OUR KUNG FU SKILLS COULD HANDLE THOSE CHALLENGES, WE CAN CERTAINLY HANDLE THIS ONE TOO.
PO?
PO!
WHAT? I'M JUST CARBO-LOADING FOR ENDURANCE.

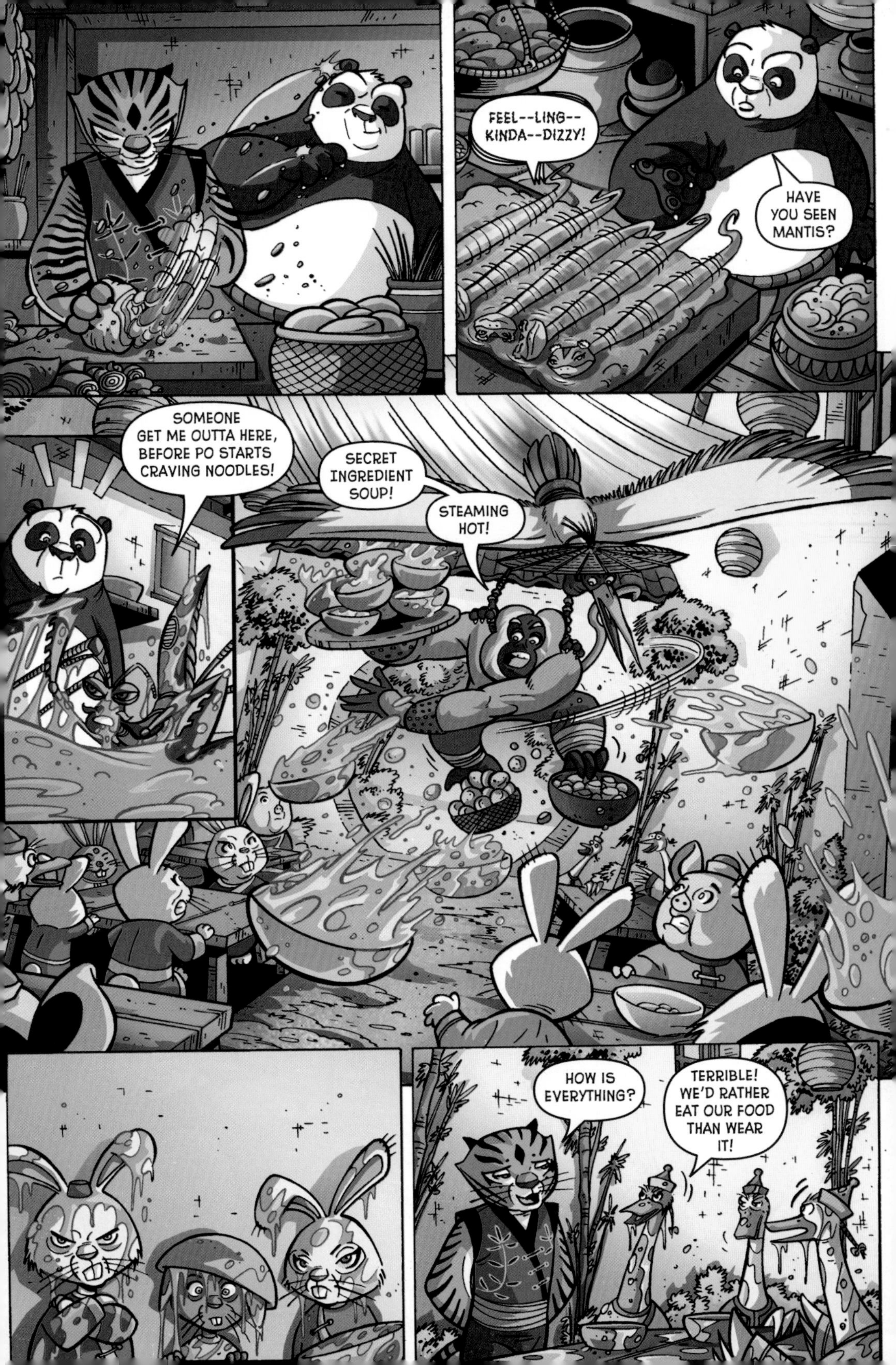
FEEL--LING--
KINDA--DIZZY!
HAVE YOU SEEN MANTIS?
SOMEONE GET ME OUTTA HERE, BEFORE PO STARTS CRAVING NOODLES!
SECRET INGREDIENT SOUP!
STEAMING HOT!
HOW IS EVERYTHING?
TERRIBLE! WE'D RATHER EAT OUR FOOD THAN WEAR IT!

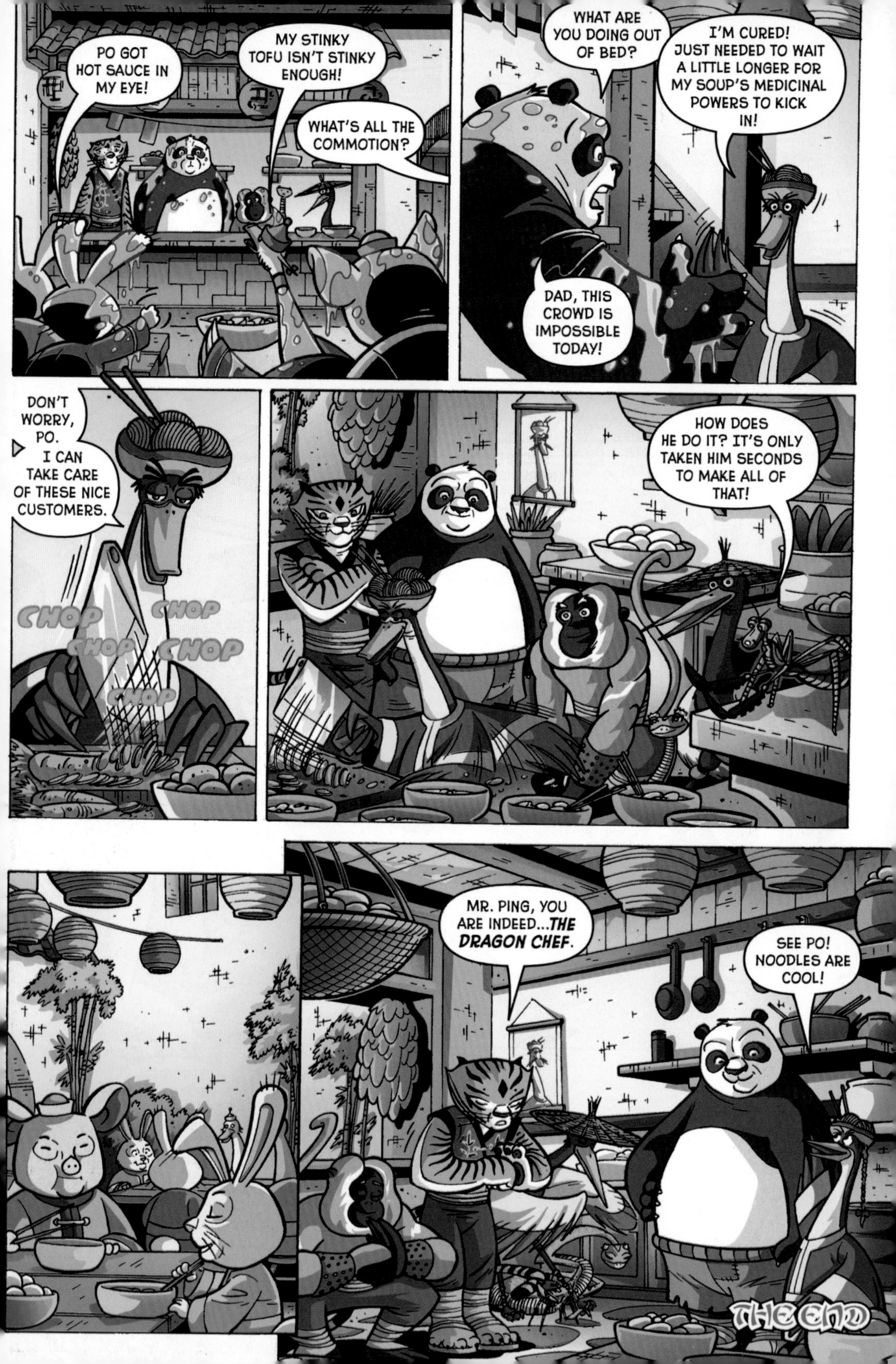
PO GOT HOT SAUCE IN MY EYE!
MY STINKY TOFU ISN'T STINKY ENOUGH!
WHAT'S ALL THE COMMOTION?
WHAT ARE YOU DOING OUT OF BED?
I'M CURED! JUST NEEDED TO WAIT A LITTLE LONGER FOR MY SOUP'S MEDICINAL POWERS TO KICK IN!
DAD, THIS CROWD IS IMPOSSIBLE TODAY!
DON'T WORRY, PO.
I CAN TAKE CARE OF THESE NICE CUSTOMERS.
CHOP CHOP CHOP CHOP CHOP
HOW DOES HE DO IT? IT'S ONLY TAKEN HIM SECONDS TO MAKE ALL OF THAT!
MR. PING, YOU ARE INDEED...**THE DRAGON CHEF**.
SEE PO! NOODLES ARE COOL!
THE END

Touch of Destiny

Story by: Quinn Johnson Art by: Chris Houghton
Colors by: Diego Rodriguez Letters: David Hedgecock

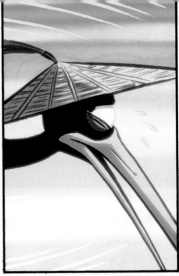

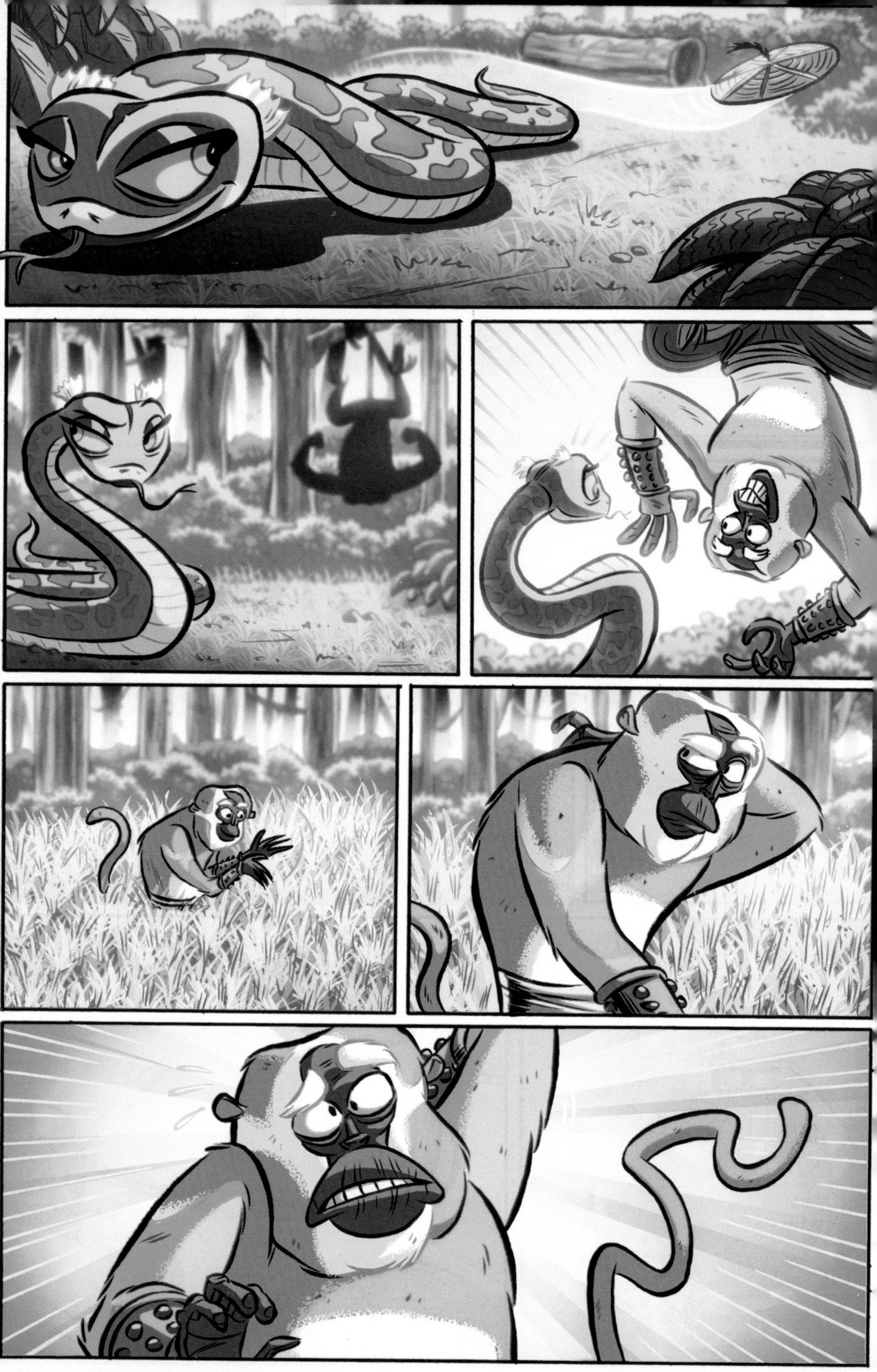

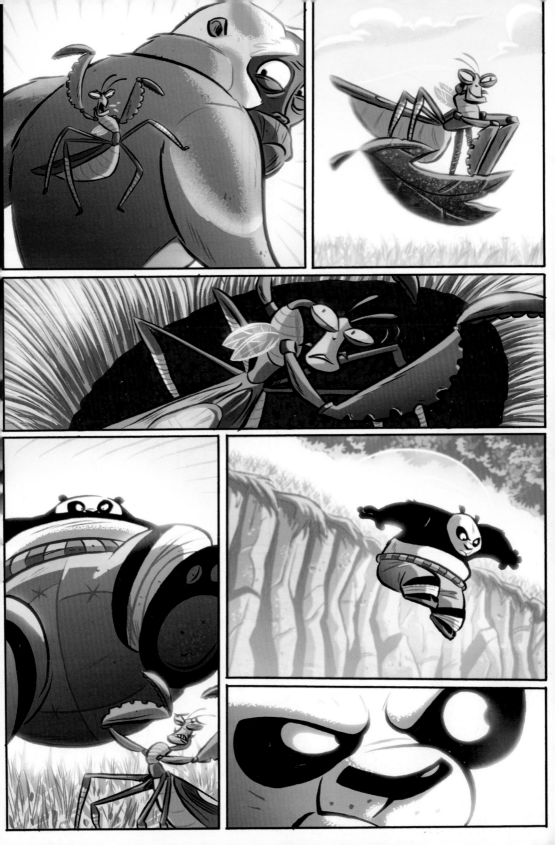

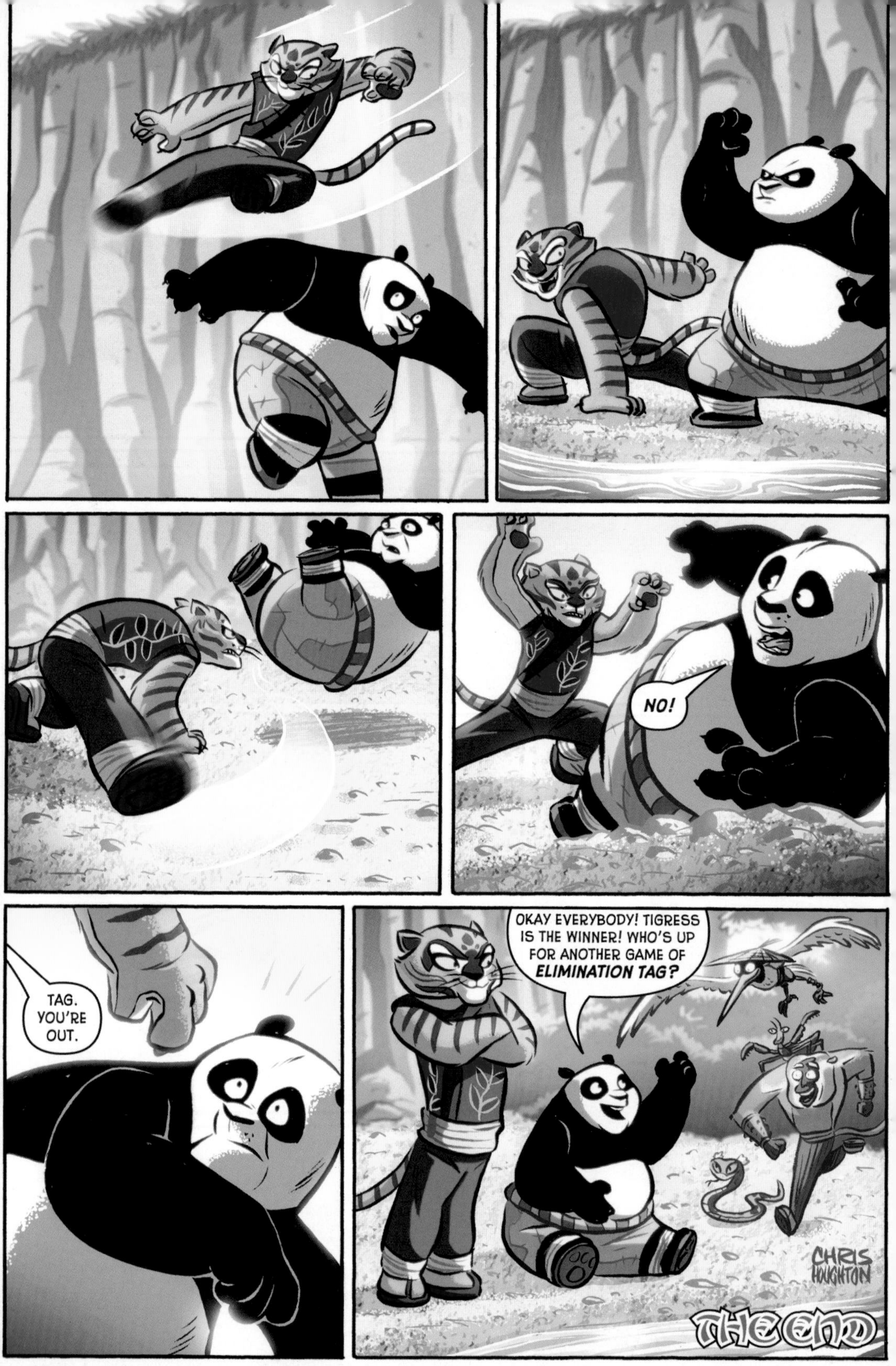
NO!
TAG. YOU'RE OUT.
OKAY EVERYBODY! TIGRESS IS THE WINNER! WHO'S UP FOR ANOTHER GAME OF ELIMINATION TAG?
CHRIS HOUGHTON
THE END

SPECIES:
Portly Panda

WEIGHT:
As light as a feather, at least during meditation

FAVORITE FOOD:
Too many to list!

SPECIAL SKILLS:
Belly bounce

ASPIRATIONS:
To have an action figure in his awesome likeness

WEAKNESS:
Stairs

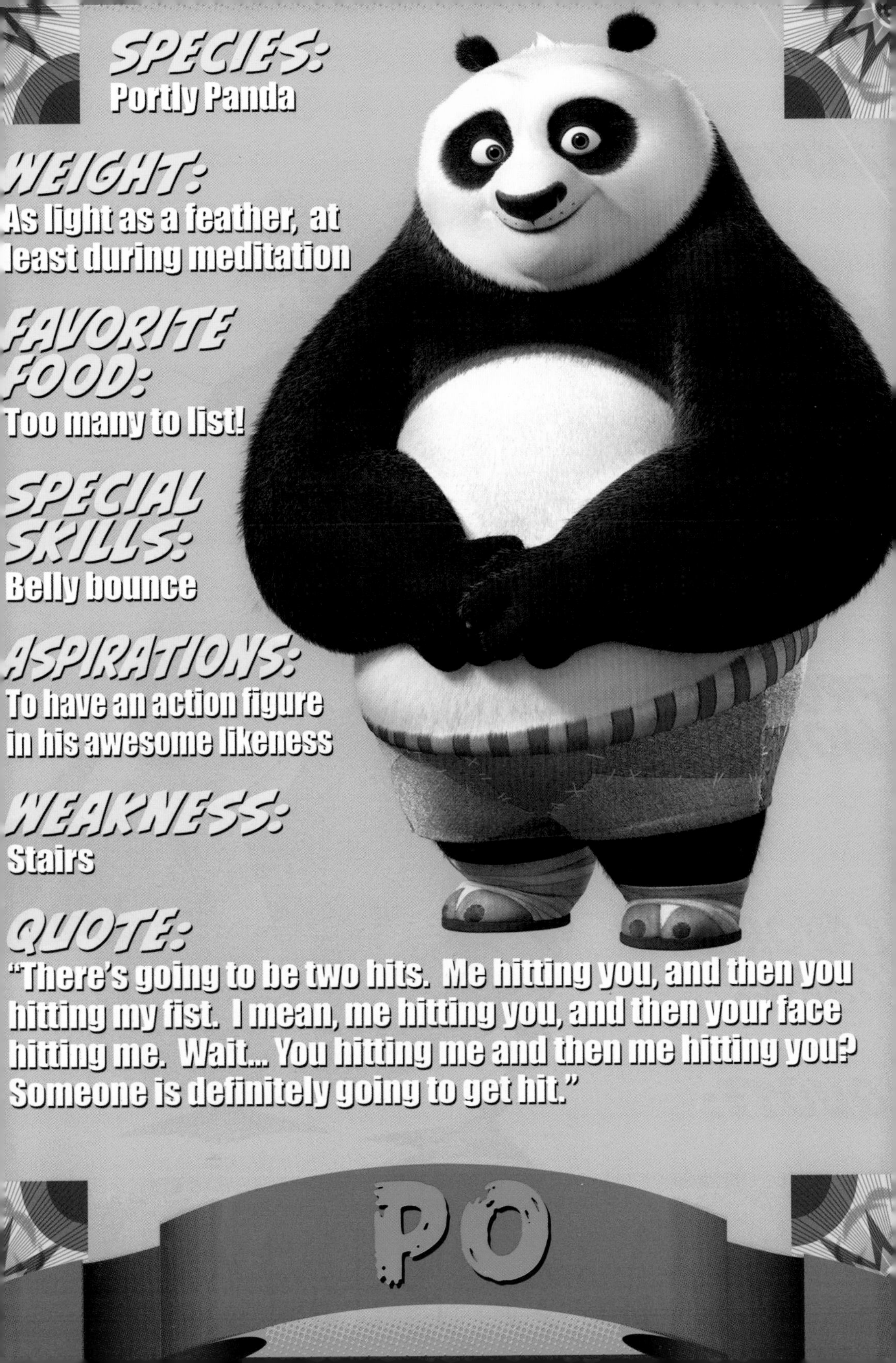

QUOTE:
"There's going to be two hits. Me hitting you, and then you hitting my fist. I mean, me hitting you, and then your face hitting me. Wait... You hitting me and then me hitting you? Someone is definitely going to get hit."

PO

ASPIRATIONS:
To expand the noodle shop internationally

FAVORITE RECIPE:
Secrent ingredient soup

LEAST FAVORITE INGREDIENT:
Duck

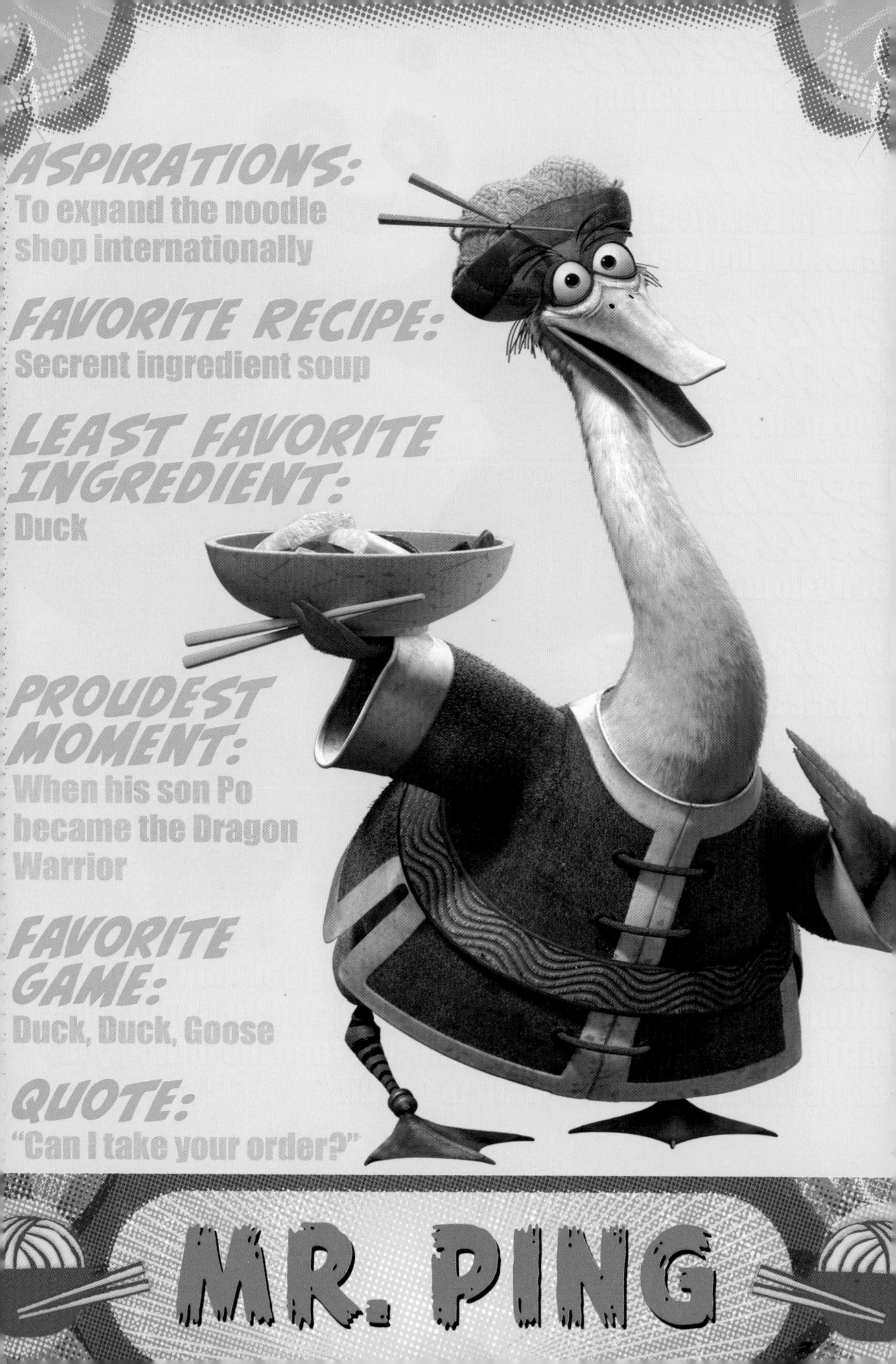

PROUDEST MOMENT:
When his son Po became the Dragon Warrior

FAVORITE GAME:
Duck, Duck, Goose

QUOTE:
"Can I take your order?"

MR. PING

GREATEST STRENGTH:
Hard style technique

SPECIAL SKILLS:
Feels no pain

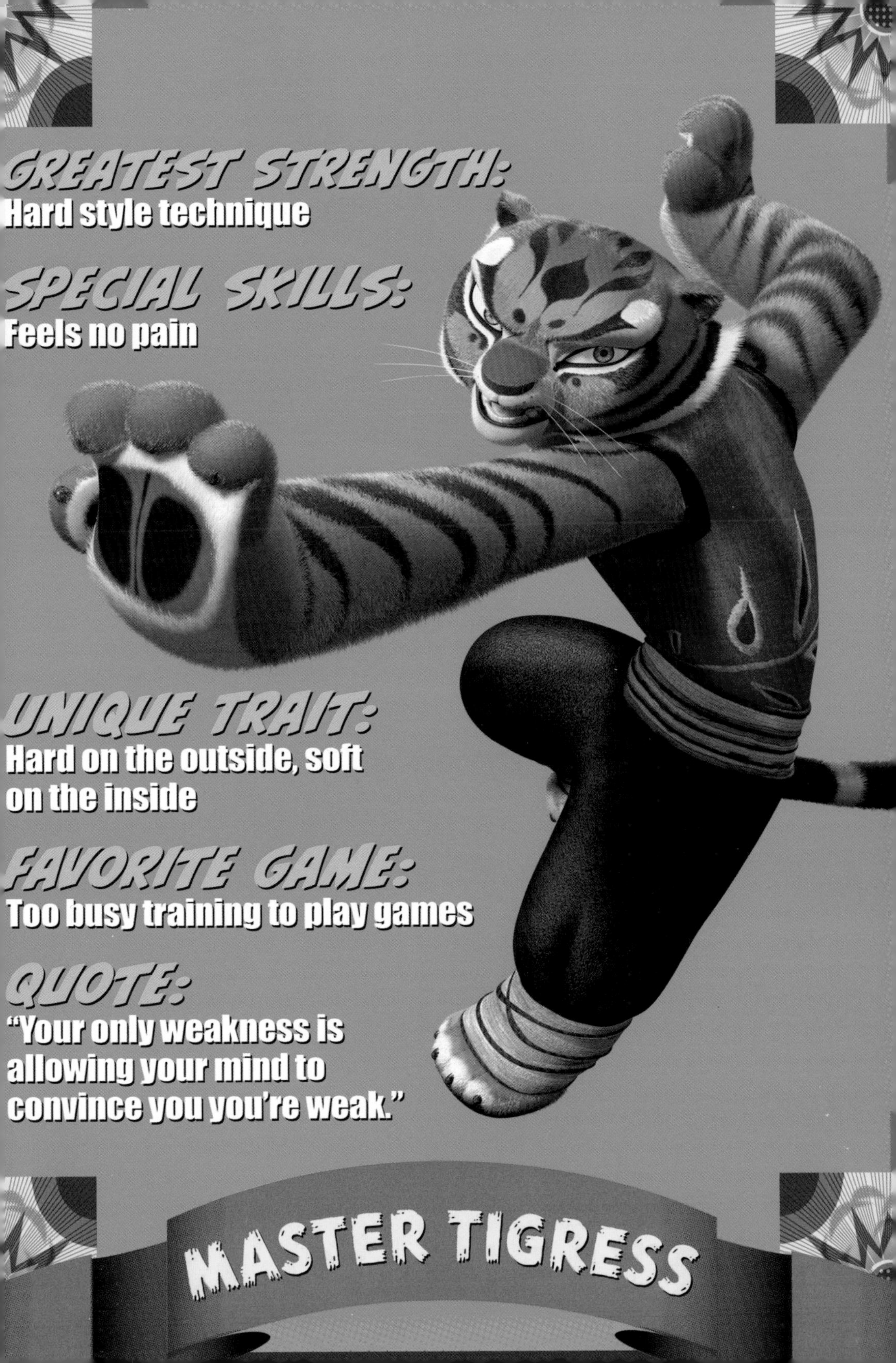

UNIQUE TRAIT:
Hard on the outside, soft on the inside

FAVORITE GAME:
Too busy training to play games

QUOTE:
"Your only weakness is allowing your mind to convince you you're weak."

MASTER TIGRESS

TRAINING TECHNIQUE:
Monkey bars

GREATEST STRENGTH:
Primate-powered punch

GREATEST WEAKNESS:
Banana splits

FAVORITE GAME:
Monkey in the middle

SPECIAL SKILLS:
Aerial ape assaults

QUOTE:
"For once I'm not the 800 lb gorilla in the room."

MASTER MONKEY

STRENGTH:
Razor sharp talons and wit

WEAKNESS:
Bird Flu

FAVORITE SONG:
"Insane in the Crane"

FAVORITE BAND:
Wings

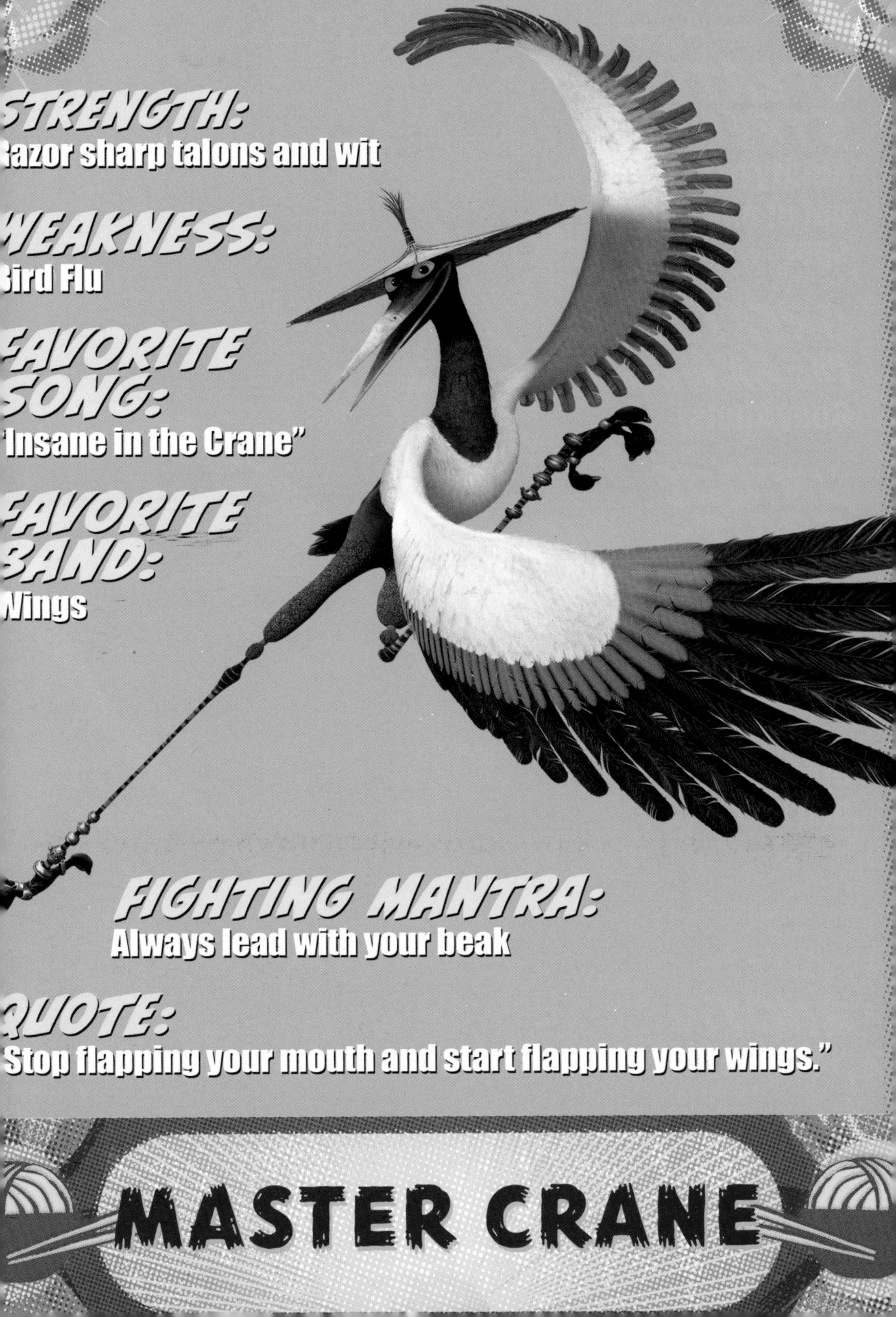

FIGHTING MANTRA:
Always lead with your beak

QUOTE:
"Stop flapping your mouth and start flapping your wings."

MASTER CRANE

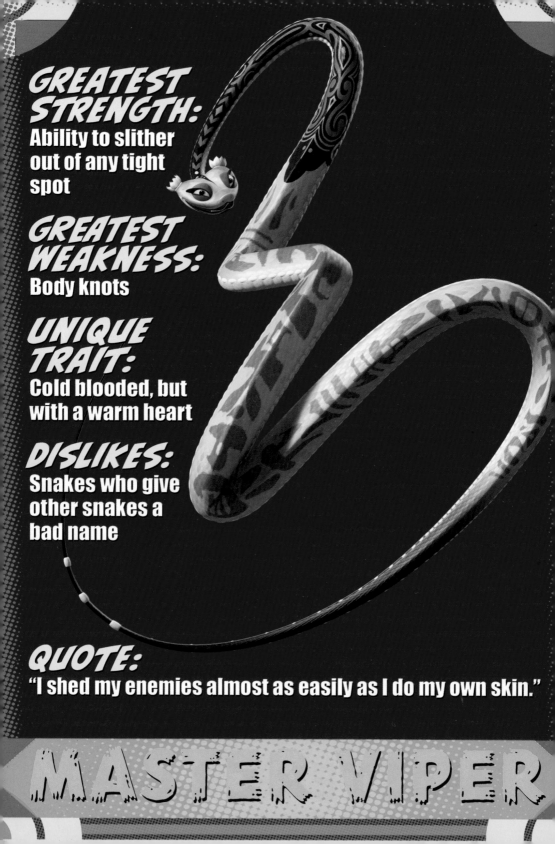

GREATEST STRENGTH:
Ability to slither out of any tight spot

GREATEST WEAKNESS:
Body knots

UNIQUE TRAIT:
Cold blooded, but with a warm heart

DISLIKES:
Snakes who give other snakes a bad name

QUOTE:
"I shed my enemies almost as easily as I do my own skin."

MASTER VIPER

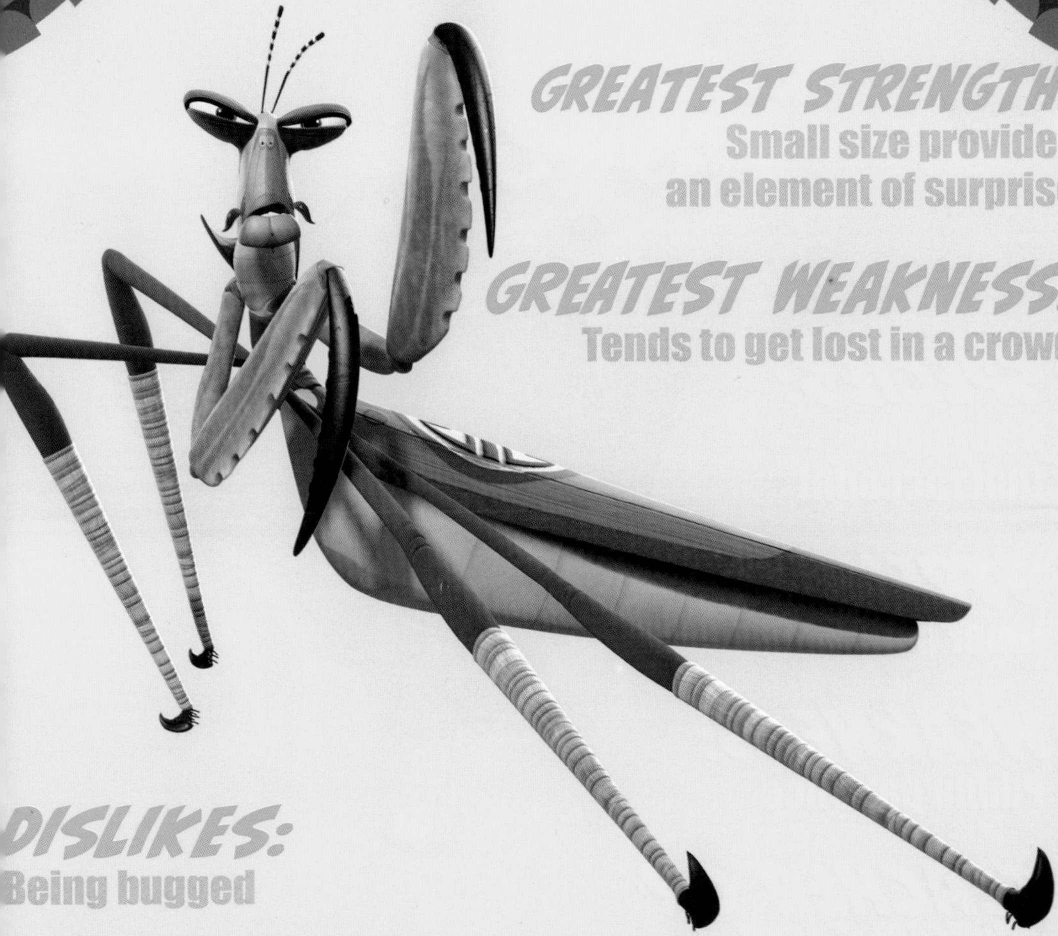

GREATEST STRENGTH:
Small size provides an element of surprise

GREATEST WEAKNESS:
Tends to get lost in a crowd

DISLIKES:
Being bugged

ASPIRATIONS:
To one day overcome his six left feet and learn how to dance

QUOTE:
"It's not the size of the insect in the fight, but the size of the fight in the insect."

MASTER MANTIS

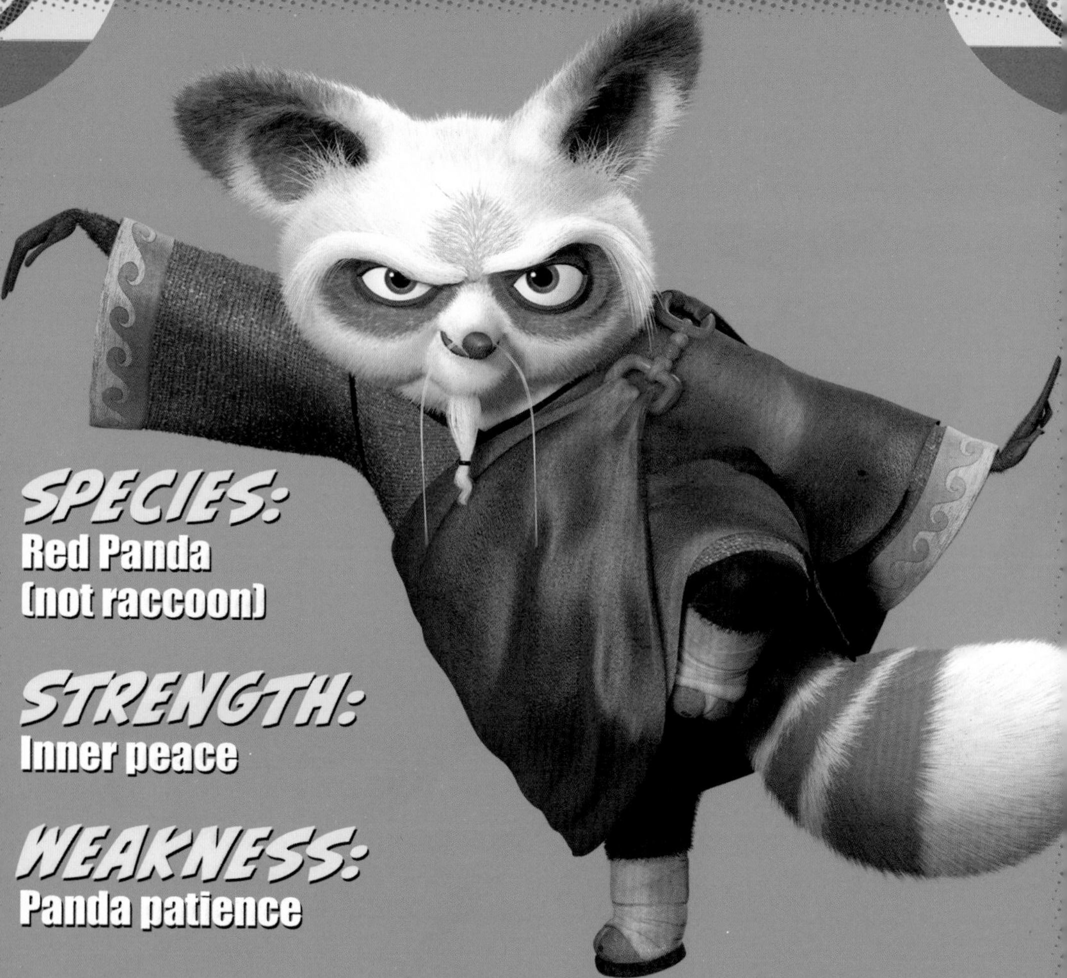

SPECIES:
Red Panda
(not raccoon)

STRENGTH:
Inner peace

WEAKNESS:
Panda patience

TEACHER OR STUDENT:
You can not teach until you've learned

RETIREMENT PLANS:
A true master retires only when time does

QUOTE:
"Again!"

MASTER SHIFU

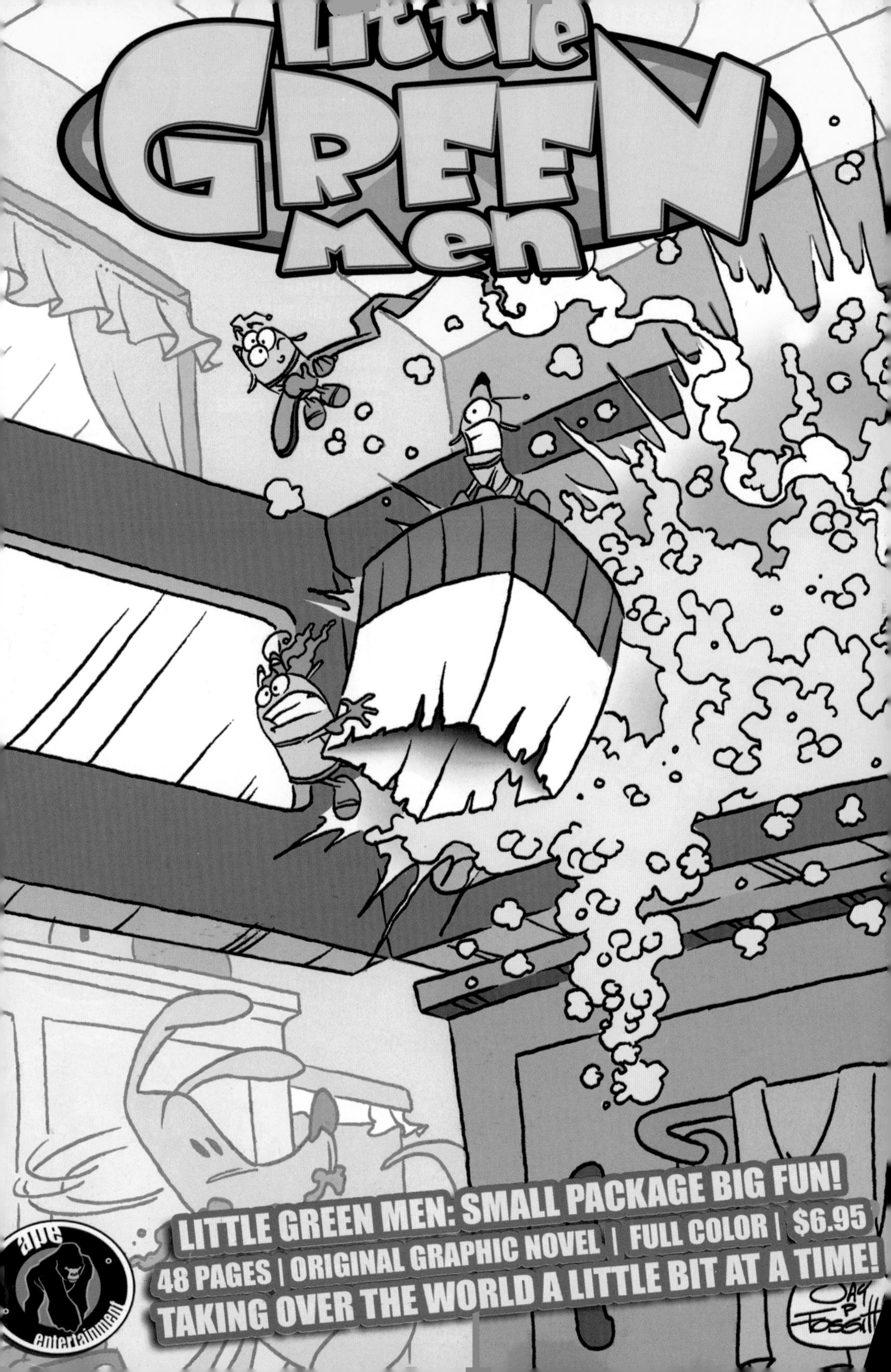

Little GREEN Men
LITTLE GREEN MEN: SMALL PACKAGE BIG FUN!
48 PAGES | ORIGINAL GRAPHIC NOVEL | FULL COLOR | $6.95
TAKING OVER THE WORLD A LITTLE BIT AT A TIME!
ape entertainment

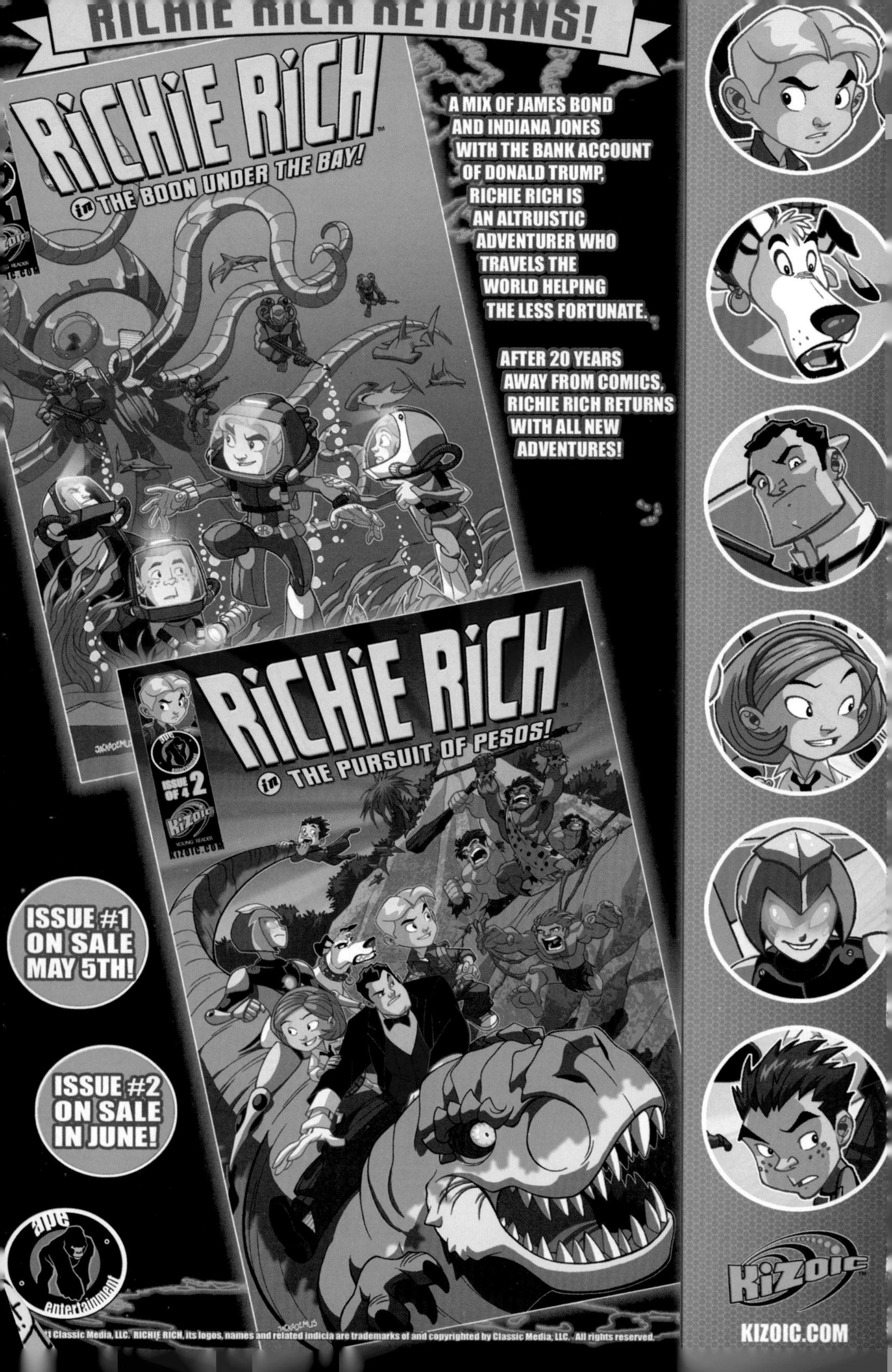
RICHIE RICH RETURNS!
RICHIE RICH
in THE BOON UNDER THE BAY!
A MIX OF JAMES BOND AND INDIANA JONES WITH THE BANK ACCOUNT OF DONALD TRUMP, RICHIE RICH IS AN ALTRUISTIC ADVENTURER WHO TRAVELS THE WORLD HELPING THE LESS FORTUNATE.
AFTER 20 YEARS AWAY FROM COMICS, RICHIE RICH RETURNS WITH ALL NEW ADVENTURES!
RICHIE RICH
in THE PURSUIT OF PESOS!
ISSUE OF 4 2
YOUNG READER
KIZOIC.COM
JACKADEMUS
ISSUE #1 ON SALE MAY 5TH!
ISSUE #2 ON SALE IN JUNE!
ape entertainment
11 Classic Media, LLC. RICHIE RICH, its logos, names and related indicia are trademarks of and copyrighted by Classic Media, LLC. All rights reserved.
KiZOIC
KIZOIC.COM